THE DAY THE CA

THOMAS HINDE is the pen-name of Sir T
born in 1926 in Felixstowe, Suffolk, the son of a boys' school headmaster. He was educated at University College, Oxford, where he read Modern History, and began writing his first novel while serving as a teacher to a farmer's two children. He worked as a civil servant and later for the public relations department of Shell Oil Company in England and Kenya before becoming a full-time writer in 1960.

His first novel, *Mr. Nicholas*, appeared in 1952 to great critical acclaim. The influential critic Kenneth Allsop called it 'one of the few really distinguished post-war novels', and it was widely praised in both England and America. Other successes followed and secured Hinde's reputation as one of the most gifted English novelists of his generation; some of the best are *Ninety Double Martinis* (1963), *The Day the Call Came* (1964), and *Games of Chance* (1965), the latter comprising two novellas, 'The Interviewer' and 'The Investigator'. *High* (1968), a novel set on a college campus, drew on Hinde's experiences teaching at the University of Illinois from 1965 to 1967. Four further novels appeared in the 1970s, followed by *Daymare* in 1980, and, after a twenty-six-year gap, *In Time of Plague* (2006). Hinde has also published more than a dozen nonfiction books. He and his wife, Susan Chitty, who is also a writer, live in Sussex.

RAMSEY CAMPBELL has been described by *The Oxford Companion to English Literature* as 'Britain's most respected living horror writer'. He has been given more awards than any other writer in the field, including the Grand Master Award of the World Horror Convention, the Lifetime Achievement Award of the Horror Writers Association and the Living Legend Award of the International Horror Guild. His latest books are the novel *The Kind Folk*, the short story collection *Holes for Faces* and the novella *The Last Revelation of Gla'aki*.

Cover: The cover features a reproduction of the original dust jacket art by Victor Reinganum. Born in 1907, Reinganum studied art in London and Paris and became a freelance illustrator in the late 1920s when he was hired by *Radio Times*. He went on to do freelance work for Shell, London Transport, British Rail, and others, and later was well known for his dust jackets, among which his designs for Muriel Spark's books are perhaps the best known. Reinganum disliked categories, but the abstract nature of his art generally led to his work being classified as 'Surrealist', and his work was frequently shown at Surrealist art exhibitions. He died in 1995.

By Thomas Hinde

Mr. Nicholas (1952)*

Happy as Larry (1957)

For the Good of the Company (1961)

The Cage (1962)

A Place Like Home (1962)

Ninety Double Martinis (1963)

The Day the Call Came (1964)*

Games of Chance (1965) *(two novellas)*

The Village (1966)

High (1968)

Bird (1970)

Generally a Virgin (1972)

Agent (1974)

Our Father (1975)

Daymare (1980)

In Time of Plague (2006)

* Available from Valancourt Books

THOMAS HINDE

THE DAY THE CALL CAME

With a new introduction by

RAMSEY CAMPBELL

VALANCOURT BOOKS
Richmond, Virginia
2013

The Day the Call Came by Thomas Hinde
First published London: Hodder and Stoughton, 1964
First Valancourt Books edition 2013

Published by Valancourt Books, Richmond, Virginia
Publisher & Editor: James D. Jenkins
20th Century Series Editor: Simon Stern, University of Toronto
http://www.valancourtbooks.com

Library of Congress Cataloging-in-Publication Data

Hinde, Thomas, 1926-
The day the call came / Thomas Hinde ; with a new introduction by Ramsey Campbell. – First Valancourt Books edition.
pages cm. – (20th century series)
ISBN 978-1-939140-58-6 (alk. paper)
1. Spy stories. 2. Suspense fiction. I. Title.
PR6058.I524D39 2013
823'.914–dc23

2013023370

The publisher is grateful to Mark Terry of Facsimile Dust Jackets, LLC for restoring the copy of the dust jacket used for this edition.

Set in Dante MT 11/13.5

INTRODUCTION

'I LIKE TO REMEMBER THINGS MY OWN WAY . . .'

LET me declare my interest from the outset. I first encountered *The Day the Call Came* back in 1966 and was both dazzled and disturbed. It was in the Corgi Modern Reading paperback, a splendid series now so forgotten that there appears to be no account of it on the Internet. As I recall I first became aware of the imprint when I encountered its edition of Nabokov's *Pale Fire*, a book I no sooner saw than bought. Like Penguin in those days, Corgi Modern Reading seemed to guarantee books worth having, and they generally were. Few of them rewarded me more than *The Day the Call Came*, and I've often been delighted to acknowledge my debt to it as a writer. Not long after I read it I had a stab at emulating its method in a short story called 'The Lost', and I believe I've subsumed its influence in some recent comedies of paranoia – that's how vital it remains for me. It belongs to a mode that Kafka may have invented and Rex Warner subsequently developed, but in this novel as well as his novella *The Investigator* Thomas Hinde finds it a highly individual voice and brings it into a world that is still contemporary. Indeed, he might be writing about one that is all the more with us.

Nothing is more crucial to the effect of *The Day the Call Came* than its style. Perhaps the narrator is as unreliable as any of Poe's, but his tone is far more chilling and insidious. He doesn't need to assure us that he is being reasonable, because that's how he sounds. We can't even feel we know more about him than he does, given his interludes of lucidity. One insight the book offers is how sane the deranged may appear, even often to themselves. We may sense that he's at least as intelligent as we are, and more devious in pursuit of his secrets. Indeed, late in the book he reflects that 'you can do a lot of suspicious things under people's noses' because 'even if they notice their minds busily fit reasonable explanations to them.' It's both an indication of the way he deals with people and an inadvertent description – a projection, in fact – of the way his own mind plays tricks on him.

The prose is as lucid as the summer sunlight in which many of the events take place. (Not for nothing is a later Hinde novel called *Daymare* – a good term for quite an amount of his work.) We may be surprised by how the ominous first line leads to a lyrical celebration of the landscape, a passage that gives way to a hallucinatory glimpse, hinting how insecure the narrator's vision really is. His thoughts of his children subtly suggest how his viewpoint always turns inwards: the fairy-tale giant that has lodged in his mind from his childhood, the way he perceives their behaviour in terms of his own at their age, his refusal to have them at home (a prohibition that, we may feel, his wife has accepted too readily, unless – like so much else here – that's merely how he sees her response). The memory of the giant seems less simply nostalgic, more menacing, when it's followed so closely by another image that could be a child's fantasy – the houses that 'hadn't moved yet'. Late in the novel a dream of 'healthy fluffy bunny' rabbits turns as hideous as any child's nightmare.

At times the prose has the glancing quality of the uncanny that we find in M. R. James. Even a tense may be ominous. Hinde's later novel *The Village* offers tours de force of the pluperfect, but in *The Day the Call Came* a single use can imply a great deal: 'I'd liked my family . . .' We may learn to watch out for words too. When our narrator says that he has overheard a neighbour 'drawing other people into conspiracy with her', perhaps the observation is less innocent than the context would have us believe, or is his paranoia infecting us? The spy's eye that's trained on everything around him is as keen as any in the genre that had come to the fore at the time – we may think of the obsessive detail to be found in Len Deighton's espionage novels of the same period – but the kind of detail on which Hinde's narrator fixes (or fixates) sets him unnervingly apart from his companions on the contemporary shelves. Not least the jokes, some of which are hilarious, convey a sense of a skewed view of the world: see the entrance of Percy Goyle's dog, for example. Even the most apparently objective sections of the narrative can't help betraying the nature of the narrator in some aside or other – his having 'failed to trace' an aspect of a neighbour's background, for instance. We may suspect why his wife sometimes grows frightened when she can't find him, and wonder why the sight of his daughter playing on the lawn should give him indigestion. Some of what we learn about him – his name, his age – feels like information he has only inadvertently let slip.

The incident of the typed letter seems to offer a route back to sanity, but the narrator gets lost along the way. Each of his forays into apparent rationality falls victim to his inflamed intelligence, which is too cunning to take even his own thought processes at face value. One of Hinde's achievements in the book is to render episodes simultaneously comic and, in terms of the observer's conclusions, disturbing – see the splendid episode of the Draycotts' preparation for their camping trip and the developments that follow their exodus (developments that may begin to make us wonder which of the events we're told about have actually taken place: do the Draycotts actually return so soon?) It's when the narrator turns his suspicion on his family, however, that we're reminded that this may not be a comedy at all.

As he grows more devious, so does the narrative and in particular his belief in his own rationality, but he can't help betraying himself to us when we're as trapped inside his head as he is. A passing observation about the traffic he encounters on a family outing is enough to suggest a whole history of hidden paranoia. I confess that, as the offspring of a schizophrenic, I may be uncommonly conscious of familiar symptoms – the assumption that someone has been 'worked on', the aircraft that's identified as belonging to a watcher (both persistent beliefs of my mother's) – but this novel is liable to make any reader uneasily alert. As the social comedy grows wilder, so do the deranged observations it provokes. When the narrator becomes obsessed with the notion that his neighbours are sharing secret jokes about him, we might think the laughter he overhears is our own, however nervous.

The last stages of his disintegration intensify both the comedy and the nightmare – the inappropriate remarks he inserts into social gatherings, the absurd denials with which he confronts his family, the disguise he dons – but the dark humour (even of the horrendously hilarious visit to the Brightworths) can't camouflage the terror. The novel ends with that, all the more powerfully because so much is left unsaid and, worse, imminent. The fiction of Thomas Hinde is long overdue for appreciative reappraisal, and this book is a fine introduction. When I was asked to contribute to the horror volume of *The Book of Lists* I included it in my survey of great horror novels not usually regarded as such (along with books by Peter Ackroyd, John Franklin Bardin, Samuel Beckett, Patrick Hamilton, José Carlos Somoza and others). It did occur to me that readers might not be able to find some of them, but now in the case of *The Day the Call Came* they can. May this new edition lead to a revival of his work.

RAMSEY CAMPBELL
Wallasey, Merseyside

June 9, 2013

THE DAY THE CALL CAME

PART ONE

THAT was the day the call came. It came without warning. For years I'd known it would come, sooner or later. I'd got used to knowing it would come. I'd stopped expecting it.

There'd been nights when I'd woken and gone into a sweat at the thought that at any moment the telephone by my bed might ring. They'd got fewer.

It might not come by telephone, of course. They'd never told me that. But I thought it would. The radio transmitter-receiver which I kept in my attic, hidden below three loose floorboards – somehow I'd never quite taken that seriously. Even the two-monthly checks . . .

There'd be no danger. I'd only have to lift the receiver and say yes and yes. There'd be no confusion or doubt. I'd lie there, propped on my elbow, listening and saying yes, wide awake as I always could be the instant after sleep, my mind racing ahead, calculating the problems. I wouldn't have to ask questions. They'd never give orders which needed amplifying or could be misunderstood. And afterwards I'd invent some story about a wrong number or a madman to tell Molly – if she'd woken. That was how I'd imagined it coming.

It didn't come like that.

It came in the evening. I'll tell you what I'd been doing that day.

It was the first day of my children's holidays. I was glad it was going to be fine for them. On and off it had been fine for a week but that was the first day I felt certain. At dawn it had that stillness, bright but not too bright, which you get when an English summer suddenly arrives. It was in no hurry. It was going to be fine not just today but for many days.

I stood on my back drive, sometimes watching for the sun to rise over the hills, sometimes looking down at the mist which still hid my orchards in the low lands. For a long time nothing changed, then it was quickly getting brighter, as if someone was making a dim-up on a stage machine. Several inches above the hills where I hadn't expected it the sun came through the mist, round and yellow. At the same moment I saw that the mist was thinning below me and row after row my trees were coming into view. Beyond them I could see the common and the golf course.

My orchards were out of place in that part of the country. I suppose they used to be a paddock and a couple of meadows belonging to some farmhouse which had disappeared, land where the farmer could bring his cattle in winter or when the lord of the manor was stag-hunting on the common. They stuck out into the common like a promontory. From here above them I could see clearly the neat green rectangle made by my leafy trees. The sun was lighting their tops. Beyond and to their right I saw the bracken and broken silver birches of the common. The sun was lighting these too. To their left I saw the sandy bunkers and yellow gorse of the golf course. The sun wasn't lighting these yet.

The rest of the morning is less clear, but I must have gone to my attic to work till breakfast. After breakfast I must have sat in the farm office, as I usually did at that time of day. No doubt I paid some bills and read some catalogues. Probably I went over the argument again about how I was going to handle the crops that year – though I think even then I'd decided.

Perhaps it was the weather, or perhaps I'm casting back the flavour of what happened later on to what went before, but I seem to remember feeling restless that morning. I needed to go out more often than usual and walk about the sunlit lawn before I could clear my thoughts and make decisions.

Something worried me, but when I tried to trace it I couldn't. It was less a feeling of worry than a feeling that I ought to be worried.

One small incident stands out. I was half-way across the lawn to the azaleas on the descending bank where it ends. I was watching a grey squirrel which had clamped itself to a pine trunk, perfectly still, thinking I couldn't see it as I certainly shouldn't have done if I hadn't noticed it scurry there, when something made me turn and look at the house. I saw Molly passing a window. A fraction of a second later, before she had fully passed it, she saw me and turned rather suddenly and opened the window to lean out.

She smiled. 'Isn't it lovely!'

'Isn't it!'

Now at the second before she'd seen me and turned I'd noticed that she was climbing past the window and deduced that she was going upstairs. And it wasn't till we'd spoken like this and I'd turned to stare with her away across the low lands to the distant hills of heather and blue sky that I recovered from the shock of what I'd thought at that second: that the stairs she was going up were not those from ground to first floor but those from first floor to my attic.

It only lasted that long, and the actual moment of doubt a shorter time. Yet it should at once have been clear to me that she was on the lower stairs. True, the windows were in the same vertical line, but as well as being at different heights they were of totally different shape. The only explanation, and it wasn't satisfactory, was that some dazzling effect of the sunlight on the glass had prevented me from seeing the other window, ten feet above the one she was passing.

It wasn't satisfactory because I was less concerned about how I had made the mistake than why.

My attic was private and Molly never went there.

'This should worry them,' she said. She referred to a joke of ours that most of English industry and commerce was geared to cold damp weather so there was tremendous pressure against letting us have anything else. It may not be a joke. 'Don't forget the train.'

'Twelve-forty?'

'I'm not sure,' she said and shut the window.

My attic was private because it had always been agreed between us that she mustn't disturb or – till it was ready – try to see my work.

It was because of my work that Molly never expected me to show much ambition about the farm. My farm was too small to be very profitable unless I'd done something intensive like chickens. One day I was going to be successful but it would be no thanks to my thirty-three peaty acres of English soil.

It was also perfectly understood between us that Molly asked no questions about my work. The times I had been nearest to telling her, the times I had felt my love for her persuading me that this was more important than anything else, had been when I had come down from my work and seen how badly she wanted to ask about it, but wouldn't let herself. I'd seen anxiety in her eyes.

More often, because it had become habit, she hadn't wanted to ask.

I don't remember whether the idea of my work was my own or whether they suggested it. It has been convenient. In the early mornings and again in the long winter evenings I would go to my attic. Molly expected it and would have been uneasy if I hadn't. It gave me all the time I wanted for my training. Sometimes I had bought materials for my work and, once or twice though not too often, I'd left the bills for these lying where she would see them.

Though it was perfectly understood that Molly should never go to my attic workroom, and though I trusted her completely, I kept the door locked when I was elsewhere, and locked it when I was inside.

I met the twelve-forty. This year the breaking-up day of each of my children's schools was the same and I'd arranged for them to meet in London and catch a down train together. Molly stayed at home to cook lunch.

She was boiling a pudding. She made good puddings, in an old-fashioned way in a cloth, which we called 'giants' heads', because the position of two raisins had once looked like two eyes. It was the sort of inspiration Molly had and as soon as she'd said it I'd seen that it did look exactly like the round pop-eyed head I'd always imagined on the pot-bellied giant who smells Jack hiding in the copper. Sometimes I thought that the shout her children gave to hear that it was giant's head for pudding was the most concrete moment she looked forward to in their holidays. I don't much like puddings.

They were hopelessly excited. Though they had been together for an hour in the train they both talked without stopping or listening. They seemed pleased to see me but only as an extra, sometimes forgotten, audience.

It was funny to hear them. Although Dan, who was eleven, snubbed everything Peggy, who was nine, was saying, I felt he only did it to make space to tell his own things. And though Peggy was being snubbed she hurried on to the next, hardly bothering to defend the last. It was the sort of exchange I'd heard end with her suddenly saying, 'Oh you're horrid,' and bursting into tears, though this time she didn't. They'd not yet learned to be ashamed of their excitement and hide it. I thought they were backward, but I was pleased. Perhaps they hid it at school but could not stop it breaking out when they saw each other.

I remember how the sun shone that afternoon, making me narrow my eyes and glance for shade when I came out to see what they were doing. They couldn't decide.

They couldn't decide if they wanted to be in their rooms or in the garden. Or whether they wanted to be together or apart. Or which of the things they'd thought of doing in the months they'd been away was the thing they most wanted to do. It made me remember how I'd felt on the first day of my own holidays.

I remembered how I'd known that to go on hesitating would destroy the happiness I'd hoped for and that I must decide to what to devote these holidays – sticking in all my stamps, making a *Beau Geste* boat with gunpowder guns – because there had been holidays when I'd put off this decision and realized too late that too many days had already been wasted.

Seeing their uncertainty made me sorry that I had to send them away to school, which must be a bad place if it prevented them doing so many things to which they could have brought hope and enthusiasm. Molly had hated their going. There'd been no argument. I couldn't remember ever having to explain to her how they would disturb me if they were always at home. But I'd seen how she wished they could stay.

Peggy wanted to make a garden. Dan wanted to build a house in a tree. Dan wanted his house to be finished and belong to him. He wanted practical help which he could then forget. The achievement was the object. Peggy wanted to watch me digging and then to be watched while she dug and then for us to dig together. It was the doing she cared about.

I helped them. And I persuaded them to try to learn tennis. We had a rough grass court with some rougher netting to stop the balls. It suited Peggy better than Dan. Peggy wanted to be able to tell people about how she was learning and I was teaching her. Dan wanted to start the game and win.

As the afternoon grew hotter I became more anxious to sit and rest. I envied our cat which I could see lying under a rhododendron bush in the black cavity between the bottom leaves and the ground – and then couldn't see because it had taken the chance while I was looking away to slip into a safer place. Dan and Peggy didn't notice the heat.

After tea I went down the hillside path to the orchards. I liked to go down there at least once a day, even when there was little to do.

That was why I'd chosen fruit farming – again I'm not sure if it was my idea or theirs – though Molly would have liked some stock. At times of the year I was busy from dawn till after dark, but at others I could take days or even weeks for my real work. It all fitted. I had made these important decisions soon after I joined; and that was soon after we were married, so we were able to take them together. I joined when I was twenty-three.

My fruit farm kept me fit, but not exhausted. More important, it kept me on the premises, because I never knew at what hour and how urgently I might be needed. That was why, besides the telephone by my bed there was an extension in the main orchard shed and loud bells outside the back door and on a post by the orchard gate. I'd explained to Molly that one couldn't afford to miss deals in such a competitive business.

Down in the orchards I lost sight of the common and golf course, though I still had the feeling of being on this green rectangular promontory. When I looked back and up I could see the roofs and chimneys of the houses on the New Lane. They were all different, of course. Mine was about the centre and the tallest. With its red tiled mansard roof it was about the ugliest.

Once I had hated that row of houses. They had had a flavour of Wells' monsters from Mars, and seemed to look down on the country they were going to move over. Later I hadn't minded them. That still summer evening I almost liked them. Perhaps I had been lulled into security because, in eleven years, they hadn't moved yet. From among them, fainter than seemed likely so that I couldn't have told exactly from where, I could sometimes hear the sound of tennis ball on racket but interspersed by too much high shouting for it to be a proper game.

I came up the hillside path. I crossed the front drive and lawn. I went through the french windows into the sitting-room. At once I saw it on the mantelpiece.

It was propped against the back wall, but it wasn't conspicuous. True, we didn't usually prop letters on the mantelpiece, but it wasn't alone there. Apart from the black striking clock and the two silver-plated candlesticks there were several ashtrays and six of Molly's ornamental cups and saucers – strange how she's come to like these ornaments which her mother and mine would have liked but which I'd assumed she never would. In spite of these, and of the filigree china pot which was holding it up and hiding one corner, I saw it at once. I hadn't a second's doubt about what it was.

It had a presence, that small brown envelope on my sitting-room mantelpiece. I stood watching it, a little warily, as if to suggest that despite my complete acceptance it should have used more tact. No doubt the shock gave me this instinctive defensive feeling which I didn't ordinarily have. There wasn't a sign of how it had got there.

In that second when everything seemed to stop I became aware of what everyone else was doing. Across the lawn on the tennis court I could hear Dan and Peggy. 'No, no, no, NO,' I heard Peggy call and then a pause when I could imagine them making faces at each other. Upstairs I could hear Molly singing and because of the day of the week and the occasional rustling of paper I knew she was unpacking the laundry. Glancing back through the french windows I could even see our cat – or at least its tail as it made its way carefully through the bottoms of the azaleas a foot beyond the lawn's edge over the crest of the bank. Its tail moved like a sail, sometimes pausing and twitching. And here was I, alone in my sitting-room with that envelope.

A second later I was beyond the sofa and had it in the inside pocket of my jacket, only able to notice as I hurried it there that it was addressed to H.C. BALE in typed capitals and nothing else. I couldn't read it here.

My problem was where to read it without causing suspicion or being seen. Six o'clock wasn't my time for going to the farm office, still less to my attic workroom. I'd just come from the orchards and could hardly go again. There were trees and bushes in our garden, which was half wild, and even a fir plantation at the far end, but wherever I went there was a chance I might be discovered, and I'd taught myself not to take chances. So I kept it in my jacket pocket.

I tried not to think about it and for half an hour succeeded but at supper in the kitchen I got the idea that it had begun to work itself out of my inside pocket and was showing between my lapels across my shirt front. I thought that was why Dan had begun to stare thoughtfully at a point below my collar bones.

'Daddy,' he said – and I had a moment of panic when I could think of no answer to the question I expected – 'do they really gut cats to make rackets?'

Molly protested. Peggy blocked her ears, showing that it had been meant for her, and began to chant, 'Dan, Dan, the lavatory man.' Dan got up to hit her. In the confusion I was able to glance down. The letter wasn't showing and, casually slipping my hand inside my jacket, I felt it safely in the pocket.

At about nine when the late dusk of the summer evening was coming I went upstairs, noticing through our bedroom doorway and out through its window the dark red and purple sky where the sun had set. I went up the second flight and sat in my attic chair. I took out the envelope.

I couldn't learn much from that. It was pale brown manila, the sort of envelope half the businesses in the country use for their bills and receipts. I had some myself. I slit it open.

Inside was a single white sheet. Typed a little above the centre, not in capitals, were the two words 'Stand by.'

Just that. On a sheet of quarto without a watermark, typed by a portable typewriter with an élite face, of rather old-fashioned design, a pre-war Imperial I'd have said at a guess – oh yes, I'd done my training.

I won't deny that I felt let down, even angry. All right, I wanted to say, but for God's sake tell me what it's about.

Steady there, I said to myself. No hysterics.

Before I went to bed I thought of fetching my long-barrelled .38 with the silencer and putting it under my pillow, at least of going to the safe in the cellar which I'd built behind the wine racks to check whether it and the others were there and in good order. But I knew they were.

And I wondered whether I should call them and send the 'message understood' signal.

I didn't do a thing. I knew that was what they would want.

I went to bed and made love to Molly. I think she liked it. She gave several quick gasps and I was pleased that I was giving her pleasure – distantly pleased.

Several ideas came to me in the night. In the morning I woke with them complete in my mind but no memory of how they had arrived. I went to the attic and fetched the letter.

I'd thought when I woke that I'd been wrong about the weather and there were grey clouds but now I saw that it was the clear grey of the sky before the sun rose. It was rising now and from the stair window I saw it shining through the fir branches. The children's doors were shut and there were no sounds inside. Yesterday had been exhausting for us all.

I took the letter to the farm office. The envelope, as I'd realized at once, might have come from my own packet. The paper, as I'd now guessed, was similar if not identical to the watermarkless make I used myself. I'd guessed that the typewriter was an old Imperial portable and mine was an old Remington portable. I bent and examined the desk closely, but didn't touch it because I had the idea of taking a dusting for fingerprints on its polished edge and on the typewriter keys. I could have done it – but there wouldn't have been any. And what was the point?

I had to admire their efficiency. Not a thing had been moved since I'd last been there after lunch the day before. The catalogues and farm letters were in their neat piles. The chair was pushed back to exactly the distance I always pushed it and set at the angle I always set it to get out. When I sat at the desk I didn't have to move the machine an inch towards me to adjust it to the distance I liked. I took out a sheet of my quarto and typed, 'Stand by.'

I folded the sheet three times and held it side by side with the one I'd been sent. I couldn't see a single difference. Soon I wasn't sure which was which.

There were no inked-up letters, but there was something funny about the descending strokes of the 'y's. I examined them with the magnifying glass. It was the final proof that the note had been typed on my machine.

PART TWO

It was late that evening, as I was tapping the barometer in the farm office, that it occurred to me that I might have typed that note myself. The idea seemed to float into focus as if I had been half seeing it all day. You may think that once I had recognized it I should have been able to accept or reject it at once. It wasn't so simple as that.

True, I was able at once to *think* I could remember typing it, but that proved little. To start with, even if I had done it, then why had I done it! But more important, if I could ever have completely forgotten doing it, how could I trust myself now that I thought I remembered doing it? There had been a moment when that action – if it had been an action – had not existed for me. How did I know that I wasn't now inventing it? Because if I could invent it I could also invent the intervening period of continuously remembering it. I had noticed how my dreams would provide not just people but a memory of things about them from long before the dream began. For instance, a dream in which I'd known that Molly had been the second of two twins and one half of her hadn't come out properly – one half divided vertically. And that this was why that half was wrong, or just more darkly shaded, I can't describe it any better. In my dream I had not only known this but known how it had affected the whole of our life together. I could have described in detail an infinite number of events from that past life.

In the same way I now *thought* I had always known that I had typed that note. It proved nothing. As I stood there tapping my barometer – it was rock steady above thirty-one so that I could give it several extra taps – I didn't have to work this out. It was just an example of my suspicion that one's memory was selecting all the time and for this reason there was no such thing as what had 'really happened'; that was something we invented because of an anxiety to believe ourselves real. I had another reason for being unsure.

When I joined they didn't have to tell me that for security reasons my memories of the actual mechanics of those early contacts must be suppressed. And this didn't mean buried where they might be dug up, but set into competition with other memories, a competition which because of their superficial improbability they would lose. I found it fairly easy.

I was able to invent incidents in my past and elaborate them and after a few weeks become genuinely unsure whether or not I was remembering what had happened or what I had thought about so carefully that I now believed. And even when something seemed to obtrude as a real memory, by remembering it and rethinking it I could make it not more but less real because any real memory there might have been was obscured by the process of remembering it.

You may say that's absurd, because I could have confirmed the facts in a dozen ways, by asking Molly or other people I'd known.

The first trouble here was that the sort of facts I wanted confirmed were ones which only I had ever known. But even if I'd wanted to reassure myself by using ordinary examples, what answer was I likely to get if, for example, I said to someone, 'Tell me, my father was called William, wasn't he? And this does look like a genuine letter I had from him when I was a child, not one I've forged? And he was killed in a car crash when I was ten?' Their answers would aim off in many directions, to protect me from myself and protect themselves from contact with someone so odd – and that would be even if I could believe I was actually there in front of them, questioning them, a thing I'd come to feel less sure about. And even if I'd got some sort of corroborative evidence from them and believed it at the time, how could I know soon afterwards that this was real and not an idea or so-called invention of mine? On the contrary, I could be sure that I shouldn't know.

But of course there were moments when I thought that I could, if I wanted, work out so-called real from so-called unreal, and moments when in a sort of panic I wanted to. Once I'd even made a chance to talk to Molly about the past by taking her to a place which I remembered as important to us both: the bar at Victoria where I'd asked her to marry me.

I hadn't been there between that time and this visit, and as soon as I went in I was trying to fit the place I was seeing to the place I remembered. It seemed so different that I wanted to go out and hunt for another though I knew there could only be one in this corner of the station.

'Let's be romantic,' I said. 'Same corner.' I was hoping that where we had sat, beyond the bar's angle, I would find something more familiar. I'd taken half a step in that direction before I realized that she'd been shifting her weight to move in a different direction. She stopped herself and followed me, and didn't mention it, but I saw she was worried.

Of course I knew that bars could be redecorated and their whole lay-out altered. I told myself this as we reached the table. It was fairly reassuring.

'Keep my place,' I said. 'And I'll fetch them. Two gins and French, wasn't it?'

'Oh no, beer,' she said. 'You always had beer.'

'Did I really propose on beer?' I said, making it funny. I didn't feel funny, because those two gins and French standing there on that dark brown polished table had been clearest in my mind when I'd thought about this moment. In those tulip-shaped glasses. And the way I'd stared at them and moved mine about to make a pattern of wet rings. I even thought I remembered giving myself hearty advice to look up because it wasn't the gins I was proposing to.

'That's right,' Molly said when I came back with one for her and a half of lager for myself. 'And you upset yours and it ran off the table into someone's shoe. And you said something . . . Yes, you said . . .' But she couldn't remember, and anyway I was hardly listening. I had absolutely no memory of the incident.

Could it possibly have been part of such an important occasion and I had entirely forgotten it? We seemed to start to hunt together for things we could both remember which would prove to us that this half-hour had really happened.

I expect we found some. I expect I was able, by a little cheating, to convince her. Myself, I was only convinced that whether or not it had begun as one occasion it was now two quite separate ones. Or rather, four, because there was the one I knew and the one she was telling me about, and the one she knew and the one she was hearing me tell her about – unless of course these were mine as well. I could see them starting to multiply like images in facing mirrors. I saw that the more I went on thinking about them, the more they would multiply and confuse me. I saw another possibility, that Molly had known all along that no proposal in a bar at Victoria had ever happened but hadn't dared to tell me.

But if so, why had she invented unnecessary and absurd incidents which I would be certain not to remember – unless she was thinking it was all a joke, had been trying all the time to make me admit that I had brought her here as some elaborate funny joke.

Perhaps that attempt of mine to verify the past had been particularly upsetting. Certainly I hadn't tried again. And nor could I afterwards see things that had happened in the same solid way. My belief, like other people's, became interspersed with long periods of doubt. That quiet summer evening, staring at the rock-steady barometer needle, I felt doubt about that note. I registered it, but I didn't fight it. I'd learned that that was best.

For a week nothing happened. My children enjoyed their holidays – or rather I decided they must be enjoying them on such long sunlit days with only small far-up clouds, though I realized how typically adult it was to simplify their feelings in this way. And Molly – what did she do? Cooked for them, telephoned for more food, occasionally made their beds.

She had a special way of coming downstairs which told me that she had been up to make their beds and after pulling one back and looking at it and then out at the blue sky had decided that it was a bad way to spend her time. I could tell by the way she aimed to go past me without speaking till she saw me watching her and then gave me an uncertain smile as if unsure what I had guessed. How long she spent in the house and how little she achieved always surprised me, and I think it was because she did things with a minimum of efficiency. She would start everything from supper to a drink of orange squash as if it were to be a party and to consider the cost in confusion would be to insult the spirit of the occasion. She got things into the greatest muddle in the shortest time and only later and very slowly put them straight.

In the garden it was the other way. I was always amazed by how much she made grow with how little effort. She would poke plants into banks and they would flower and spread. By occasionally bending and pulling she kept her beds free of weeds. I hardly ever remember her setting out to garden – in gardening coat or gardening gloves. More often she seemed to be watching, admiring, encouraging.

That week, perhaps because I was noticing things which over the years I'd ceased to notice, I was surprised that this life made her happy. If it was because of her hope for my ultimate success, I should have felt burdened by it. I hadn't felt burdened. And over the years the chance of my succeeding had receded, become something we had agreed to believe on a special level of its own. What else could explain her contentment? That she was a dull, easily contented person? Easily contented perhaps, but not dull. She was intelligent in an intuitive way, clever at bringing arguments to support her beliefs though not at forming beliefs from her arguments. I got no further with it.

Once or twice that week it occurred to me that Molly might wonder what made *me* contented – but then, *I* had my work.

And occasionally I was saddened by what was going to happen. Though I wasn't yet certain what this would be, I already realized that afterwards nothing would be the same. I'd come to like this quiet life more than I'd intended.

I'd liked my family. I'd liked my house with its views over half the heather-topped hills in the county. Especially I'd liked it on early mornings in summer when they were still asleep.

Sometimes I'd left my attic to go down to the orchards, particularly in budding time to keep off the bullfinches. That was a good enough reason. I'd taken my old four-ten, but I'd only once shot one. That may sound odd, but it's true. Why? To start with they're one of the prettiest birds I know. And then the businesslike way a pair of them work – in half a day they can strip a tree – busy but somehow quiet so that unless you look carefully you see nothing except occasional bits and pieces dropping to the ground. And then there won't be any bullfinches soon. But I doubt if these were the real reason. I think it was the sight of that one I'd once shot.

By chance a couple of pellets had carried off the lower half of its beak. There was just a bloody stump. I didn't like that. I suppose it made me wonder how I should feel if it happened to me. If in a war or after some explosion I put up my hand and instead of a lower jaw there was a soft wet space, so that I knew no doctor or hospital could ever give it me again.

I went down there on several perfect early mornings that week. As the days passed there was less mist and they dawned sunny from the first. I went there on purpose because I wanted to know about what I might lose. If there was a choice I wanted to understand it and know that I had chosen right. I don't think there was a choice.

On the seventh day we went to supper with the Brightworths. We knew several of our neighbours well enough to ask each other to meals every month or so and even to call unasked and be given drinks. I'd made it my business, for reasons you can guess, to know what happened around us, but it had been pleasant too. Of all our near-by friends I liked Jim Brightworth and his wife Janie best.

Janie was French so I don't think her real name can have been Janie. She'd probably adopted that at the same time as Jim.

'Oh, come in there.' She was short and dark and pretty for thirty-seven and denied that she spoke English with an American accent. 'How can I? I never met any of those guys.'

I don't mean you could see she'd been pretty ten years ago. She was still pretty, in a full-faced girlish way. I knew she was thirty-seven from things she'd said which I'd added up, in particular from Hubert. Hubert was twenty and she'd had him before she was eighteen.

'How are you then? Have a drink. Where's that bugger Jim?' To us Janie was always warm and friendly. She at once drew us into a conspiracy. Together we were laughing or angry or in despair about all the other tiresome people around. I'd sometimes been surprised to overhear Janie drawing other people into conspiracy with her.

'Is he home yet?'

'He's home all right.' She opened the drinks cupboard which

at the same time as opening downwards in front thrust itself up at you from inside. The first time I'd seen this whole shelf rising towards me I'd stepped back quickly, thinking it was going to tip a dozen bottles on to my feet. It held at least twice that number.

You could ask for any drink and Jim would provide it. Once when I'd said Carpano and he hadn't had it I'd seen him a minute later writing something on an envelope; and when he'd seen that I'd seen him he'd laughed and said, 'Not going to let that happen again.' It was funny, but not too funny.

'Well, take a look at that!' Janie said, as if seeing what she'd revealed with fresh-eyed wonder. She left it open – I had to pour the drinks myself a moment later – and came and sat on the wall-bench. 'Gee, I'm glad you came first.' I think she really was.

The wall-benches were foam rubber, tartan covered and set along two walls which met at an angle of thirty-five degrees. Between them was a triangular table, also with one angle of thirty-five degrees, with ebony black top, splayed legs of quarter-inch brass tubing and ball feet as big as polo balls which looked like iron. Janie had a way of sitting on her wall-benches, with her feet forward, her shoulders against the wall and a large gap behind the small of her back, as if making them look as uncomfortable as possible.

The first time I went to the Brightworths' house it was still new and she'd asked me how I liked it. I already knew that she and Jim had planned it together and Jim had taken six months off from his business to build it. Looking round its sitting-room, with no wall or window the same size and a sloping ceiling, I'd said I liked it a lot. I do like contemporary design.

'It stinks,' she'd said sadly. And then, pointing angrily at a single lemon yellow tile set at stomach level in a jet black wall, 'What's that, for Godsake? I mean what *is* it?'

Presently Jim came. He was over six feet, with a big sharp nose. He had earth on his shoes and something grey like cement dust in his hair. I remembered that Jim was building a swimming pool.

Of course labourers were doing it for him. They dug, transplanted hedges and wheeled barrows of concrete while he supervised. But I felt that when Jim was down there he was one of them, totally involved in the work. Down there, making his pool, he was like a burrowing mole.

When he was with you he'd agree to come up and look around at the change he was making in the landscape. He'd even taken me through the trees to visit it. And he'd made modest, deprecating noises, which were perhaps half genuine because he may have had doubts. But I'd known these were needing his imagination and he could only with an effort understand what it must seem like to me. He was a believer talking to a heathen.

Every week-end and every evening when he came back from his business he laboured at it, but I think he half realized that he didn't want to finish it, let alone guess what it would be like. What he wanted was to be down there, burrowing. When it was finished he'd have to find a new burrow.

'Hallo, all,' Jim shouted. I could see he wanted to give me a playful blow on the shoulder, but was stopped by the clay on his hands. 'Helping yourselves! That's right. We like go-ahead friends. Pushing, that's what you've got to be.'

He stood watching us, grinning, using the back of one hand to rub an itch at the point of that sharp, but at the same time solid, triangular nose.

Other people began to come; supper was to be a buffet barbecue. As I've said, I'd taken an interest in our neighbours, and knew enough about most of them to surprise them. You can imagine that I was particularly watchful that night.

First there was old Percy Goyle, who collected butterflies. He wasn't a professional. He just liked them. I wonder why I say old, because he was only twelve years older than me, forty seven or eight, I'd forgotten which. He felt old.

Of course he'd occasionally written letters to lepidopteric or natural history journals, but not to attack or propose general principles. He'd written – I knew because I'd traced some – to offer specific facts about butterflies and moths he'd seen in his own garden. (There had been several in a correspondence about which species chose to settle in direct sunlight.) I might have guessed this from the way he'd talked about them when he'd first shown me his collection.

At some party soon after I'd met him I'd asked, in a spontaneously interested way, if he'd let me see it, and he'd agreed – with a slight hesitation which I'd thought was modesty. So next day I'd gone and quite soon I'd made some remark, borrowed from a recent broadcast, about the myth that butterflies lived for one day, and how it had arisen when it seemed to us obvious, not only because of their migrations, etc., etc. I think he knew the answer but he didn't say. He'd had an idea that I might be interested in butterflies in the way he was interested in them, in watching them in his garden with wonder or delight, or something else – I still wasn't sure. He realized that he was going to be disappointed. He wasn't snubbing and soon we were talking on an easy superficially scientific level, but the way he'd listened and not answered had told me what he felt.

It had even occurred to me that he might wish we still believed butterflies only lived for one day.

Though I'm no expert, I'd guessed that his collection was remarkable for one made entirely within ten miles, and without night lamps.

'You actually caught all these?'

He nodded.

I imagined him, knee deep in summer grass, net raised, wondering how it had escaped. 'And set them yourself?'

'I used to.'

He'd left me with them and stood at a window, looking out across his lawn. His house was only one away from mine, though the trees hid them from each other, and must have been built about the same time, but it had a different feeling. Mine was open and light, so that from one side I was often able to see through its various windows to someone who was doing something, but hadn't noticed me, on the other. It felt frail, as if its brick walls were thin. Percy Goyle's house felt thick and heavy with a genuine Tudor gloom inside to suit its mock Tudor outside. The windows were small and around these bright points of light you couldn't see what was piled on the floor or hung on the walls. It's hard to remember whether his ceilings were artificially beamed or merely felt as if they were. When he stood that day in front of his window he cut off most of the light from the cases I was looking at. When I glanced at him he was in black silhouette against the bright daylight, but because the window was small this silhouette began at his waist and ended at his neck so that I couldn't see his legs or head.

By the year I'm writing about, insecticides and seed dressings had killed most native English butterflies. There would be summer days in succession when I didn't see one.

Money was Percy Goyle's problem, too much money. It came from Mildrew and Goyle, manufacturers of marine engines, and I didn't doubt there was a tyrannical northern industrial father to do other damage.

When I'd first seen Jim Brightworth with Percy Goyle I'd been surprised. I couldn't understand how they could have anything to say to each other, let alone any mutual sympathy, and I had often felt that I should excuse and explain each to the other. Now I felt there was no need. They seemed to like each other and as they were both my friends this pleased me.

Percy had a way of sidling into a room and standing quietly by the door, as if wanting to prolong the moments before he was seen. If he was seen at once he seemed to suffer a physical shock. He was seen at once that night.

'Come in there, Mr. Goyle,' Janie called. I was sure I saw him start. 'I don't have to introduce you to our good friends. Eh?'

He smiled at Janie and smiled at us and mumbled.

After Percy came his peke, trotting with busy efficiency, stopping and standing as if to say, 'All right, explain if you can.' It gave several sniffs and snorts, as if to imply, 'Make it relevant because I have a cold.'

Percy's peke was as assertive as Percy was quiet. Percy minded, that was the surprising thing. He was always watching it anxiously, wondering what it would do next. And when it did, I'd seen him clasping and unclasping his hands and going up and down on his toes. It was as if he'd chosen the most small-minded, hopeful, fearful, illogically passionate creature possible as an exercise in patience.

After Percy came Mrs. Willis, who admitted to fifty-nine and had a blue rinse. She was the centre of a bridge circle. Molly knew from her two art-student lodgers that she got up at tea-time and went to bed when her bridge parties ended at three or later in the morning. And instead of empty milk bottles she put out empty gin bottles. She'd always been perfectly sober when I'd seen her, but as it was her mid-morning, perhaps that wasn't surprising. I'd failed to trace a Mr. Willis.

After Mrs. Willis came the Quorums, a retired civil servant of Irish background and his wife Queenie – I'll tell you about them later; and some others who didn't seem so important at the time. Presently Hubert appeared.

Why Jim and Janie picked that name for their son I never discovered. Perhaps it was another example of Janie's insensitiveness to the flavour of English words, though I sometimes thought she took advantage of being French and having such a good excuse for misusing them. When she shocked people she made embarrassed apologies – but she was perfectly in control. It was the others who suffered. Hubert suffered.

When I saw how Hubert curled up at the things his mother and father said, I recognized the feelings I had had at his age. It was odd to understand how he felt, and yet to like Jim and Janie.

Hubert was at a provincial university. The last time I'd met him he'd told me, after a lot of sympathetic silence, that apart from the subject he was reading he was studying the human brain – old hat, of course, but by a totally original approach. He was doing it from God's point of view. If he were God, what sort of a brain would he have given man. Summarized, it sounds bad, but I hadn't thought it bad at the time.

Hubert was tall and black haired and usually looked at his feet. It was a compliment when he looked at you through his black-framed glasses. These had thick lenses which reminded me of the circular faults in diamond-paned windows and made his eyes sometimes grow large and sometimes swim.

Finally, and typically late, came the Draycotts. They'd had trouble putting their children to bed. They brought their huge golden retriever called Boodles. They had to do that, they explained, because their baby-sitter didn't dare to be left alone in the house with him.

I happened to be looking out of the window across the drive when they arrived. I saw Wilfred Draycott open both back doors of his red mini-car and stand at one and clap his hands and call 'shoo'. I saw Boodles, who was on the back seat, raise his head but that was all. To make him move, Wilfred had to duck into the car and use both hands to push.

With a lumbering movement more like a cow getting to its feet than a dog, he came out and stood in the drive, all eighty pounds of him, quite still, a plaintive look in his eyes, as if to say, 'For God's sake show me somewhere to lie down'.

After that I could hear Rene Draycott – pronounced Reeny, and short for Irene – in the hall. She was explaining to Jim how they couldn't leave Boodles in the car because he was liable to go wild and tear everything apart so could they possibly shut him in a lobby. I heard Jim make some suggestion and Wilfred say, 'Be it on your own head'. The door opened and Boodles waddled three-quarters in, stopped and turned to look back. When he did this he raised several inch-deep rolls of golden flesh on his shoulders.

The next moments were chaotic. Like a hairy arrow, Percy Goyle's peke came from below the sofa and everybody was shouting and apologizing and cursing as they were snapped at. Even Boodles was surprised into laying back his head and giving one long howl.

As too many people were involved I kept clear and watched. I saw Jim with both legs astride the peke, using both huge hands to try to pin him to the floor. And Rene and Wilfred each using their outside hands to reach for Boodles' collar while with their inside hands they tried to push each other back. And Hubert, who seemed to have got into the centre by accident, trying to step clear. And Janie standing over them shouting, 'Why won't one of you fetch a bucket for Godsake?' More involved than any of these I saw Percy, also watching. I saw his expression of pain. I saw him start forward, then half turn his face away. He was feeling the fears and angers and heroics of each person. He was feeling for Boodles and his peke. How could he interfere?

So Wilfred took Boodles home and returned an hour later,

because of a confusion about keys. It was the sort of thing that happened to Wilfred.

Wilfred worked for an advertising agency which he'd joined on the understanding that he would do market research for which he had a passion (he mentioned it with embarrassment, as if admitting to some sexual deviation), but by accident he'd been put into the display and design unit. The agency belonged to an uncle and that made it more surprising but also more typical. Wilfred had bought Boodles to be his gun dog in a local shoot which he was to be asked to join, but he hadn't been asked.

In a tiny, apologetic way Rene nagged him, 'Wilf, you did promise . . .', and occasionally he would complain back, 'Darling, if you say so, of course, but I honestly don't remember . . .' They were like the two least hormoned hens in the flock who have been put in a coop together. They weren't good at being beastly. Perhaps that was why they were liked.

I liked them. They had genuine humility. About their children, for instance, who were two picture-book little girls: they were genuinely as surprised as they were pleased when people said how pretty they were.

And about their house, which had been given them by Rene's father: instead of swelling out in confidence to suit their accidental prosperity they seemed amazed, even crushed by it. I had a picture of them creeping about, occasionally looking up anxiously to see what they would be given next.

For an hour and a half we stood drinking gin and French while Jim carried a jug from glass to glass, never letting anyone's get less than three-quarters full. There were enough of us to make a continuous heavy shout of conversation and I thought how this must contrast with the grunts and mutterings of most of our lives at home. Nothing odd in that but perhaps I noticed it more than usual because I was being more than usually careful not to drink too much.

At around nine we went out to their low-lit barbecue-veranda with the built-in grill and the antelope skull with two red bulbs for eyes. And Jim grilled chops in an apron painted with grilled chops and a genuine white chef's hat which he'd bought from a supply shop in Soho. Janie kept shouting, 'Take that thing off,' and Jim said several times, 'What, publicly expose meself!' While other people encouraged him to keep it on, seeing how much he had looked forward to wearing it.

With the food came an eating quietness. People still talked, but you could tell their attention was half on their meat and bones. They got split up and sat on benches next to people they'd already said everything to. When it finished I expected that after a minimum interval of gratefulness they'd start to leave, and this reminded me of someone else's party where I'd seen Janie deliberately sit on Jim's knees and put her arm round his neck and wriggle till he became red in the face and left in confusion to take her home to bed. But that evening, perhaps because it was Friday, with a long night and two empty days ahead, they didn't leave and gradually, as their digestions worked, they grew more lively. Janie came past and sometimes said things to provoke them, and sometimes stared at them as if genuinely astonished that they could be so boring.

About midnight I was standing by myself in the shadows at one end of the veranda. To my left Molly and Percy Goyle were talking together, slowly and with pauses, unlike most of us. She sat with her buttocks against a table and I thought she wanted to go home. Janie was beyond them, round the curve of the dark veranda, lying on one of those plastic bed-seats which fold at both ends so that I could see her legs but not the rest of her. She was trying to make Jim dance – there was music inside – and I heard Jim say, 'What, me with me corns!' at least three times. I was thinking about Janie and how she had this exciting discontent, how she would say with real desire, 'Why can't I be rich.'

At the same time I was listening to blue-rinsed Mrs. Willis, who was talking to Hubert Brightworth close on my right, and guessing the effort of imagination she was having to make to ask him about his lessons at college and the effort Hubert was having to make not to put his head in his hands and scream, when I happened to glance between them. At once I was looking through one of the veranda's inside windows into a small half-dark room.

It was lit as if through its open doorway by some light beyond.

Standing there, but out of the path of this light, were Wilfred and Rene Draycott.

They were close together, their heads bent forward. He was saying something to her. Because of the window I couldn't hear it. As soon as he'd said it he glanced left and right. For a fraction of a second our eyes met.

It may seem a small thing. I can only say that it was one of those tiny incidents which give meaning to years of half-understood experience.

They might, I agree, have been talking about money, or their children's bed-wetting habits, or something else they were embarrassed about. I knew at once and for certain that it was none of these things. My conviction was only confirmed when Wilfred bent and said one more thing to Rene before they moved out of sight, as if they had no secret and no glance had passed between us. But not, this was the important point, *not* as if it had been about something embarrassing like a leaking lavatory.

All the way home, as we went arm in arm down the Brightworths' drive across the New Lane and along our top drive, I thought about it. It was a beautiful night, cool after the hot day, with a high half moon in a sky of faint stars. Ahead our house was a dark lump except for one upstairs window which reflected moonlight. The more I thought about it the more certain I became.

Sometime that night I formed my plan. During the Brightworths' barbecue I remembered hearing about the Draycotts' camping week-end. By casually ringing them – to ask them to tennis, say – I could discover when they were going. At about that time I could casually stroll over and offer them our safari camp-bed.

I could time it still more accurately; from my attic I could see, through trees, enough of the Draycotts' drive to tell when their mini was parked by their front door and guess when it was loaded. I'd wait till I judged they'd be leaving in five minutes. And when I got there – I'd let circumstances dictate. I thought they would.

Just what I was looking for I wasn't sure. I told myself that there were things in 'The Larches' which I didn't know, which it was vital for me to find out. But as that moment of recognition receded I realized that I needed to find out whether there was *anything* strange inside 'The Larches'. I needed proof, needed it badly.

The advantage of my plan was that the camp-bed would be a visible reason for being there for anyone who might be watching. It was also the best time to work. The hour after they'd left was the least likely for anyone they might have employed to come and stoke. Whether or not they wanted the camp-bed didn't matter, but I guessed it would be too big for the mini and this would have the added advantage that I could carry it home – later.

As I crouched at my attic window on that quiet summer morning, watching and waiting, many things which had been obscure began to grow clear.

Though I'd taken trouble to know about our neighbours, this had been an exercise, no more real than the routine posting of sentries when the battle is a hundred miles away. Because till now I'd believed it would be someone passing through whom I'd have to intercept. In the week since the call had come I'd watched the papers for statesmen paying visits, remembering how a policeman had appeared at our crossroads two years before and an hour later a prince from some Far Eastern neutralist state had driven by on his way to our local airport. That policeman standing there so innocent and useless, looking at his watch and wondering if the prince was going to make him late for his dinner, had summed up a lot.

I'd even walked once or twice up and down the main road, taking a note of bushes and walls, and of which had covered retreats to woods and open country. I saw how wrong I'd been. They weren't interested in things so out of date and powerless as princes and statesmen. I saw that it wasn't even likely to be an interception of some secret man of power whose name never reached the papers. They didn't work in such a haphazard way.

I hadn't been put here on the chance that I might be useful sometimes in the next fifteen years. They'd had a reason for needing me in this part of the country, leading the life I led, knowing the people I knew. From the first they had probably guessed how I was to be used, though they couldn't tell me.

It was someone local that I was going to take care of.

Take care of? This too was a conviction which had grown unnoticed but now became complete. Over the years a series of events too insignificant to remember had made me understand what was to be required of me. The abruptness of the stand-by call, the way it had assumed that I would need no further explanation, told me that the plan had not changed.

I'd been foolish about Draycott. When I'd had local suspicions – and I'd had these too – I'd looked for the double bluff, not the man who was hiding a powerful and cunning intelligence behind stupidity but the intelligent person who was really intelligent. I'd ignored the triple or simple bluff – depending on how you looked at it. That was Draycott.

Now that I had the clue, things I'd felt about Draycott made sense. My surprise that he could bear to foresee, as he must a dozen times a day, everything that was likely to happen to him between now and dying – or at least feel its flavour. The flavour of failure. It could only be some unsuspected hidden belief that prevented him from folding up with depression.

I found my feeling for him utterly changed. I no longer liked his humility, because I could see that it wasn't humility. The things I'd liked him for – Boodles – the gift car which had to be a mini – were exactly those I now hated. I hated the way he lost his keys and was being made to design soap wrappers. I hated his servility. I felt for him what one animal feels for another who is ill or wounded. I didn't want to look at him. If I looked at him I would want to destroy him.

At eight I saw him drive his car from their garage into the open, pass behind tall firs and park by their front door, half in sight and half hidden by some silver birches. From the way its red paint shone in the sunlight I guessed it had been polished. The number of journeys they made to it amazed me.

Time after time they came with more camping equipment, as if they might have been loading three full-sized cars. Perhaps because the things they carried were often so small that I couldn't tell what they were they suggested ants who were trying to move a pile of sand a grain at a time.

Once they came out together and stood looking at it, then went together to hunt inside it. I guessed that in desperation they had decided to sacrifice something. After that they increasingly often carried things back from car to house. They seemed to fall into competition, one loading, the other unloading, doing it faster, starting to run. I guessed they had set themselves a time to leave, because without such a target they would have no sense of starting in defeat and muddle.

Could this excessively careful loading really be explained by nervousness about camping?

I needed self-control to wait, as I had decided I must, till at last one of the two little girls had been lifted in. Then I hurried.

'It's terribly kind of you.' Wilfred was embarrassingly grateful. If it had been possible he would have taken it whether he needed it or not, but the car was totally full. Tents, sleeping-bags and pillows overflowed from the back, which was packed to the roof, into the front. Close against one window I could see the golden curly head of one little girl but no sign of her body or arms. She had a fixed look, as if she had just been woken from sleep. I couldn't see the other. Rene, in front, was sitting on a pile of rugs so that her head was close against the roof and forced forward on to her chest. In this position she had turned it sideways to peer at me through the top inch of the window. I thought something might be preventing her from turning it straight again.

It was all their own work. Alone and with no vindictive outside interference they had spent two hours working themselves into this condition.

'Don't worry,' I said. 'Just an idea. Seeing you loading made me remember it.'

When I said this I saw Wilfred start and turn his head as if it was a shock to be reminded that I could see down into his drive and he must check the window so that he wouldn't forget again. I distinctly saw him stop this movement.

'It's not that we've got any camp-beds,' Wilfred said. 'But . . .' He gave a weak laugh. He looked at my feet. He didn't look at the car. It was too shameful.

'Make it tough for them,' I said. 'Maybe they won't ask again.'

'Maybe,' Wilfred said, but not hopefully.

'Have a good time,' I said.

'Thanks.'

'You've got lovely weather.'

He looked up as if surprised to see it.

I realized that he was waiting for me to go. It could have been politeness: in his own drive he was host and mustn't abandon a guest even if an uninvited one. Twelve hours before I would have accepted the explanation. Annoyingly, the longer he waited the politer he was being, while the longer I stayed the more rudely (and surprisingly) I was behaving.

'Happy thunder storms.'

He grinned and watched me as I strolled away up his drive.

I went as far as the bend before I glanced back. He was no longer by his car but ten yards away, turning the corner of his house. I wasn't surprised.

Whatever he did there didn't take long because I was only a short way beyond the bend when I heard the car door slam and the engine start. A moment later they lurched past. They waved and I waved.

I waited till they were through the drive gates on to the New Lane and I'd heard them labour up through two gears, the second with a grind of cogs which hurt my teeth, before I stepped into the bushes.

I laid the camp-bed in a hollow and sprinkled it with leaves. Using cover I made my way quickly back towards the house. I had no time to waste. It was easy going because their garden, like the others off the New Lane, was chiefly birch scrub where it wasn't uncut pine wood.

I had an instinct to see the side of the house where he'd made that quick return when he'd thought I wasn't watching, the sort of instinct I like to follow in this work. I watched it now from a rhododendron thicket. There were various closed windows, one of frosted glass, set in walls of grey pebble-dash. Directly ahead, about four yards away across a small square of concrete, was the pea-green side door. It looked deserted in the sunlight. Had he gone back to make sure it was locked?

Under a stone by the doorstep was a piece of paper. I strained my eyes but the angle was too acute.

Ten seconds later I could read it. By that time I was half-way to undoing the lock. I stood close to the door, wearing cotton gloves of course, working by feel, looking down at that piece of paper. 'Monday one pint ONLY please.'

I was certain that he'd gone back to leave it. But why, I reasoned, should he want to do that at the last moment, when it was apparently a normal domestic message. The only explanation was that to his wife it wouldn't seem normal, because they'd already agreed to place some other order – or because they didn't order milk in that way. It was a coded message, which he could safely leave because no one – except his wife – would think it odd.

I stood in the kitchen, the door closed behind me but unlocked, working this out. Likely as it seemed, it meant abandoning the theory that he and his wife were working together. The moment when I had seen them in that dark room at the Brightworths' speaking in that secretive way must have some other explanation, and it was from that moment that my suspicions had started. I didn't decide. I stored away the two theories side by side. There was no time to decide because I had begun to hear noises.

They made me run with sweat. I didn't mind. A good internal drench of adrenalin makes me operate better. I don't take credit for this; it's just good luck. My mind goes at double the speed and in the two seconds after I'd started to hear these continuous scraping, rustling noises I'd already slipped a hand into my pocket for my gun, remembered and congratulated myself that I'd decided to bring my knuckle-dusters which were safer, quieter and usually more accurate, and checked with myself that the last thing I should do was start the fighting.

At the same time I'd been through five or six theories of what it might be, from the chimney sweep – no van in the drive – to a trapped starling. The likeliest was some cleaning woman, and I was ready to tell her how the back door had been open and, not knowing she was here, I'd come in to write a message, when I saw the door from the kitchen to the front of the house start to open. It opened slowly. Twice it hesitated, stopped, then started to open again. My grip in my pocket tightened.

The alarming thing was that no one was opening it. When the

gap was about a foot and a half it stopped completely. I could see beyond it down several yards of cream passage. They were empty. More alarming, I could still hear obscure scraping and breathing noises. I remembered Boodles.

I cursed him. He was already right into the kitchen but from where I was standing he'd been hidden by the kitchen table top. I got my fist out quickly after that to give him a knock on the head which would quiet the deep-throated watchdog howling I expected him to start at any moment. He didn't.

He just went on watching me and soon I knew that the moment of danger, if there'd been one, had passed. I still hesitated about giving him that quieting knock but decided against. This was a bad miscalculation, but seemed reasonable at the time. I don't like unnecessary cruelty.

As soon as I started to do the job, working quickly and thoroughly, I suspected that I'd been wrong. Instead of returning to sleep in some hairy corner, or collapsing where he was, from the effort of being on his feet, he followed me. And he watched. He stood in the doorway of each room I went into, watching me as I turned over papers, tapped walls, felt under upholstery, opened drawers. He got on my nerves.

Twice I led him back to the sitting-room, where on evenings when we'd visited the Draycotts he'd slept continuously on the fire rug, and tried to make him lie there. He let me take him to it, then followed me away again. I didn't like to shut a door, not being able to guess the effect of frustrating such an obsession.

I'd just returned after the second of these failures to the Draycotts' bedroom with double bed, rose-pink paper and lace curtains, and was looking into Rene Draycott's fitted wardrobe of hanging dresses – as soon as I'd opened its flimsy door I'd known that Wilfred had made it because of its mis-sawn struts, nails which had been bent at the head and ill-fitting panels which let in wedges of light, though the outside was glossy cream. I was staring at this with surprise because I hadn't known that Wilfred was a handyman, feeling an instinctive anger at this new incompetence, when I heard a car in the drive.

They'd forgotten something. I was astonished that I'd not

expected it. Voices in the drive, the front door opening, feet on the stairs. I stood frozen. I stepped into the hanging cupboard and pulled the flimsy door shut.

Despite the chinks of light from Wilfred's horrible carpentry it was dark in there. My head was among the dresses and they felt thin – diaphanous is the word – and smelt of old scent and sweat. I shuddered. At the same time I had the uncomfortable thought that Rene might need something from this cupboard. Or that they might have given up the whole camping holiday and be going to settle down to live here with me inside their cupboard. And anyway, what would they think of Boodles standing in their bedroom staring at the place where he'd last seen me?

Already they were coming nearer along the upstairs passage and, more as a reflex than because I thought it would help, I edged deeper into those stale, scented dresses. Among them I found something hard and scratchy. For a second I thought it was important till I recognized the feel of a dried orange stuck with cloves.

Perhaps it was my preoccupation with this, or with the sudden discovery that the dresses had changed to clothes of heavy material which must be Wilfred's suits, and my instinctive hesitation at breathing among these, which made me fail to concentrate for a moment on sounds in the room. I wasn't sure if they were still in it. I wasn't even certain whether they'd come into it.

Into this complete silence and uncertainty I heard Wilfred say, 'Don't do that'. It wasn't particularly loud, but shockingly close, so that I knew I'd have heard any small sounds which had come before or after. There weren't any. It was imperative but not hopeful, just the normal way he would say it, admitting a two-to-one chance it would provoke the opposite reaction.

It seemed to come from about half-way between my cupboard and the doorway of the bedroom. I couldn't tell which way he was facing. I couldn't tell whether it had been said to Rene or Boodles. Neither of them answered.

And that was all there was. Soon after, I heard doors shutting, the mini's motor starting in the drive, a grind of gears and they'd gone.

Had they known I was there and chosen not to let me know they knew? I couldn't guess.

Quickly I completed my inspection of the house. Boodles, who wasn't in the bedroom when I came out, padded upstairs to watch. I found nothing. Perhaps I didn't want to find anything else. I had enough to think about.

The back door was still unlocked. That was a relief – though of course they could have left it unlocked to quiet my suspicions. Outside the back door, lying under its stone in the sunlight, was that message. 'Monday one pint ONLY please.' It mocked me. In a second of instinctive rashness, or angry desire to punish it for its inscrutability, I slipped it into my pocket.

If I already had enough to think about I was to be given more. I'd relocked the back door, slipped into the rhododendrons, and made my way at a crouching trot through the pines and birch scrub to the point where I'd left the drive. I'd recovered the camp-bed, brushed off the leaves and begun to stroll with it towards the Draycotts' drive entrance, when I heard steps on the New Lane.

It was Charles Quorum.

Charlie Quorum was the retired civil servant of Irish background, whose wife was called Queenie and who'd been at the Brightworths' barbecue. He was heavy, with a big face the shape of a Victoria plum. Also with a Victoria plum's red stained effect, and without much hair. Because he was preoccupied he began to turn into the Draycott drive without looking along it. As soon as he saw me I noticed him start.

It was a habit of Charlie's to start when he saw you, as if your tie were missing or your fly undone, so that for several minutes you were surreptitiously feeling and checking. And if you asked, he would look astonished, so that you were unsure whether he was denying that he had started or refusing to believe that you didn't know why. Charlie specialized in uncertainty. It was his form of humour. Sometimes I felt it was more than this, that if he ever heard a complete explanation of anything, his benignly humorous pose would unexpectedly change to anger. I'd never seen it.

But I'd seen him move away from an explaining conversation, as if he could not bear to be close to it. I liked the way Charlie made conversation, just the ordinary meeting of ordinary people, into something less ordinary, always unexpected. I liked the way he refused to give or ask for explanations, and started when he saw you to make you guess. But I wondered if this particular start had been genuine. I wondered if Charlie would have preferred to be seen walking straight past the Draycott's drive.

'Hallo,' I said.

'Bale of the veld,' Charlie said, stopping and staring. He let his eyes drift once or twice to my camp-bed, then lifted them quickly away as if in pain.

'Not me,' I said. 'I was offering it to Wilfred. For his week-end.' I'd given the explanation too soon and anxiously.

Charlie didn't answer, just glanced a bit more directly at the bed.

'He didn't want it,' I said. I gave a colourful description of the loaded Draycott mini-car. 'They've gone now,' I ended, unnecessarily.

'It comes to the best of us,' Charlie said.

I smiled, uncertain what he meant.

'Ah well,' Charlie said, and went on down the drive. When he had gone a couple of paces, and without turning, he said, 'Lone Wolf Bale'. A yard or two farther on he raised one soft hand with three extended and separated fingers. Still without turning he gave a two-noted whistle of Red Indian film type and began to work his arms as if breaking into a double, but his legs went on walking.

I was still staring after him when he passed round the bend towards the Draycott house.

I was astonished that he should go there when I'd told him they were away – unless he hadn't heard. Or had I never told him but only thought I'd told him? With alarm I felt in my pocket for the piece of paper. It was there all right.

Of course there were many reasons why Charlie might call on Wilfred Draycott. He might be taking an invitation; they often went with their wives to dinner at each other's houses. Or a message for the children; Queenie took a grandmotherly interest in Rene's little girls. Or a suggestion for a round of golf; Charlie and Wilfred sometimes played together. Still more likely, he might have had hidden in his big loose jacket some map or other piece of camping advice. And it would have been suspicious if Charlie had voluntarily told me where he'd been going or why. I could imagine him continuing to go there even when he'd been deprived of his reason, simply from a habit of creating confusion. I could also imagine him coolly taking advantage of this well-known behaviour pattern.

It was true, I remembered, that beyond the Draycott back garden was the common, and a short walk across it would take Charlie to his own garden. It might even be a quicker way home. It was still amazingly cool.

I came from the Draycott drive and crossed the New Lane in deep thought. I was turning up my own back drive when I saw Molly, only a few yards away, coming towards me.

'I couldn't find you anywhere,' she said.

'Did you want me?'

'No,' she said vaguely.

I'd sometimes known her become frightened when she couldn't find me. I held up the camp-bed. I went slowly. It was easier with Molly because I knew the exact, slightly absent-minded way in which I talked to her. 'The Draycott safari,' I said. 'Offering them a comfortable night – and a few tips on water divining.'

'That's a coincidence,' she said.

'Oh?' I said. For the first time I noticed that she was carrying a jam jar with a grease-proof paper lid held on by an elastic band with some grey stuff inside.

'Taking them a few iron rations,' she said.

I guessed it was *pâté*. Molly made good *pâté*.

'Too late I'm afraid. They've gone.'

She listened to my colourful description of the loaded Draycott mini. Half-way I came to a curious halt to hear myself saying these things a second time, but I recovered and finished.

'When did they leave?' she said.

That was awkward, and I glanced sharply at her, but she was peering at the *pâté* through the glass jar as if worried about its quality. 'Just now,' I said vaguely.

'I'll put it in their frig,' she said, as if she hadn't heard me.

'But how . . . ?' I began, and checked myself heavily, sensing the many mistakes I might make.

'All the burglars know where Rene hides her back door key,' she said.

I found that answer a shock. Perhaps I was worried by the way she had watched me as she said it. Or perhaps by the way she had listened to my camp-bed explanation. Or perhaps I was shocked to realize that I, like everyone else, knew that the Draycotts hid their back-door key in the pea-green gutter immediately over their back door. I stood in the sun, thinking about it, as she went away from me, across the New Lane, into the Draycott drive.

That was the first time I wondered what Molly knew. Not once in the years that had passed could I remember her discovering anything. I didn't congratulate myself. I'd had no choice. I wondered if my care and secrecy had been enough. Had she been able, by adding up a thousand little remarks and occasions, to make an intuitive guess, to jump to the truth though the logical steps were missing?

I had a new idea: might she also have joined? Had we for years, unknown to each other, been working side by side? Had she been listening curiously to my answers about the camp-bed because this same suspicion about *me* had occurred to *her*? Was she, too, off to check the Draycott house, now there was this good chance? I felt my mind start to spin.

I came slowly up to the house. I needed peace to work things out. I went past the farm office on to the lawn and lit a cigarette. I didn't often smoke, but used the habit carefully and privately to help me think.

Dan and Peggy were reading side by side on a blanket against the house. Dan was on his stomach and elbows, his chin in his hands, his heels occasionally kicking his buttocks. Peggy was on her back with her shoulders against the wall and her book against her bent knees. They seemed unusually absorbed till I guessed it was a reading competition. Who could read most pages by lunch-time.

To start with, Molly wasn't a concealing sort of person. She was often surprised when I guessed her thoughts. But I realized that people weren't consistent. I was always discovering unexpected things about them, especially things connected with other things about which they'd already talked to me. It was as if they kept taking the covers off deeper holes. It was as if they were continuously trespassing near these holes in the hope that one day they might have the courage to lift these final covers. I'd become good at sensing when there were holes about, and encouraging them to open them. Was it possible that, because I'd thought I knew Molly better than anyone else, I'd failed to look for what she might be hiding?

One thing was certain, I must never again be so unobservant . . .

'Hallo,' Peggy called.

'Have we *got* to stay here?' Dan called.

'Why should you?' I said cautiously.

'Because of Mummy,' they said together.

'Dan's not to get lost before the doctor comes.' Peggy said.

'Doctor?' I said. I found the idea annoying. 'Who's called the doctor?'

They didn't answer, no doubt hearing my anger, unsure who it was for.

'What's wrong?' I said, making it casual.

'He's got spots,' Peggy said. Now it was she who seemed annoyed, but I guessed that was because Dan had them and she hadn't.

I was close by this time and about to ask to look when I heard a car pass below our lawn and saw it turn in at our front drive. At the same moment I saw Molly returning round the side of the house.

'Good morning,' Dr. Grott said. He was six foot two with a lot of stiff grey hair. He advanced across the lawn, carrying a bag and holding out a strong hand. 'How're we keeping?'

For a moment I couldn't answer. The phrase had a professional flavour for a fruit farmer and I wished he wouldn't use it. Also the word 'we' confused me and I wasn't sure whether he knew who was ill.

'Good morning, doctor,' Molly said, coming past me. 'I've managed to hold on to the young man.'

'Hallo, young man,' Dr. Grott said.

He squatted by Dan's rug and Molly bent opposite while Dan

took off his shirt. 'Give you a sunbath too, shall we, young man?' Dr. Grott said.

'All right,' Dan said.

'Open wide,' Dr. Grott said.

With Molly on one side and Dr. Grott on the other, I couldn't examine Dan closely but I was surprised not to be able to see any spots.

Dr. Grott stood up. 'There we are then, young man,' he said, in the wise way doctors have, hiding what they know in preparation for the times when they won't know.

I'd have liked to look at Dan myself but at this moment I was distracted by Molly and Dr. Grott, who began to walk away together. Soon I couldn't hear them. I felt again the anger I'd felt when I'd heard that Molly had called him without consulting me. I was angry with Dr. Grott for the way he had manoeuvred her on to this walk, and with Molly for going. But I didn't try to join or follow, guessing how that would hurt Molly, because her children's illnesses were her business. By the time I'd decided this Dan had dressed.

Dr. Grott drove away and Molly came back across the lawn. She smiled at me, but seemed about to go through the french windows into the sitting-room.

'What's wrong with him?'

'Nettle rash,' she said.

She stopped. For several seconds she hesitated, waiting for me to speak, but she had moved on long before I'd recovered from my astonishment. They had walked slowly for twenty yards, talking the whole time, and this was all they had said! What was more, she hadn't meant to tell me.

Molly cooked lunch and I stood on the lawn. The day was growing hotter. I began to smoke again. Beyond the empty rug where my children had been, beyond the house, across the low lands where my orchards lay, on the far purple hills I could see if I looked carefully the line of cars creeping south on the coast road. The Draycotts too, no doubt . . . Every few seconds their windscreens flashed in the sunlight. It was some minutes before I noticed that these flashes were unusual.

There were more of them than even the Saturday morning creep would make. They came and went more quickly. And they were always from the same place, a thing which might be explained by the angle of that piece of road. On the other hand . . .

But there was no need to argue any more, for I had realized that they were coming in groups. Instantly I started to note them on my cigarette packet. Two, eight, nine, six, four. After that they became erratic with flashes and pauses of many different lengths. I tried for five minutes to make a pattern of them but couldn't. Perhaps I'd been mistaken. As if in answer, they became regular again with even pauses; I counted and wrote on my packet exactly the same group of numbers.

They stopped. Several times that morning I stared across the low lands to the far hills. They didn't start again. As the hours passed I became less convinced. There were many possible explanations. It might not have been a car, but a boy playing with a mirror. Someone perhaps with a telephone number on his mind. Telephone number! I dialled it but there was absolute silence, the sort of telephone silence which seems to be waiting for something more. What more could I do?

I had almost forgotten it when I strolled on to the lawn after lunch, feeling well-fed and sipping coffee. Peggy was rolling sideways down a grass bank by the tennis court. It gave me a twinge of indigestion but I resisted calling to her – there it was again, flashing in regular groups. I didn't stop to count.

As I hurried to the farm office I guessed how it was managed: a car unsuspiciously stopped by the roadside, a windscreen which looked normal but could be slightly moved up and down by someone sitting innocently inside. It was the cleverest thing I'd seen for a long time. I got the cigarette carton out of the waste basket.

I stared at the meaningless figures.

I went back to the lawn. The flashing had stopped. I strolled up and down. Occasionally I said something to Molly. She was moving near the flower-beds, bending for dead heads, stepping back to admire. Presently, as I'd expected, it began again and I checked the same numbers. Throughout that hot worrying afternoon it went on. Irregular flashing, the message, degenerating into untidy pauses and flashes, stopping. It was still doing it as the sun went lower in the west.

At five o'clock I got the binoculars. I went to our bedroom, which looked that way, and focused them on the sunlit purple hills. Though the flashing was in its irregular phase I could see it clearly, but the exact shape and type of car it was coming from was hard to tell. This was strange because the cars beyond, still creeping on the coast road, were clear.

It occurred to me that the road and car might not be next to each other, as they seemed through the glasses, but fifty yards apart.

Presently I focused the car more clearly, but its outline and make still escaped me. There seemed to be three men in it. Oddly, the men were clearer than the car. They were wearing dark clothes and sitting upright but not doing much.

That evening, despite my worry, I was careful to go to Dan's room to say good night.

'How's the rash?'

He looked up from his book. 'Don't know.' I thought it might be upsetting him though he hadn't meant to tell me.

'When did you notice it?'

'Me?' he said. 'Not me.'

'Then who?' I began.

'How could I, in the middle of my back?'

'Oh, there,' I said, thinking hard.

'Of course,' he said with surprise.

'Was it Mummy?'

'That's right,' he said, still more astonished that I didn't know.

'When?'

'Last night in my bath.'

I knew he was telling the truth.

'Did Peggy see it?'

'I think so. I'm not sure.'

I glanced sideways, wishing I had not already kissed her.

'Let's have a look,' I said.

'Must you?' he said, but he began to sit up and untuck.

At that moment I heard Molly on the stairs.

'Oh well, another time,' I said quickly. I bent, kissed him and met her in the doorway.

Half-way downstairs, when I knew from the silence that Molly was kissing Dan and could tell from the way Peggy was calling for her that she knew it too, I came to a complete halt.

I was amazed at my obtuseness. But perhaps for an hour now I had guessed. By inserting two oblique strokes it became a date. Twenty-eight, nine, sixty-four.

I had three weeks.

PART THREE

PEOPLE don't sit in cars, flashing secret messages across the countryside on warm English summer days. I knew it as well as anyone. That hot night I broke into sweat under my single sheet as I realized it. But how could I be sure? As I've said, I had every reason to believe that I wanted not to believe it, that I had worked on myself or been worked on till I was unable fully to believe it. Still more confusing, I knew that these things did happen. Over the past years I'd read again and again in newspapers of grown-up people playing at spying in a boys' adventure story way. Of course I didn't believe newspapers. I'd never met anyone who'd taken part in any of the reports they printed and often thought that they could be manufactured as a drug by gigantic computers which fed out just enough comfort to keep people sane and just enough provocation to keep their adrenal glands active. And even if I believed them I knew the odds were millions to one against it happening to me. But I could see the delusion in that. I wasn't going to be bemused as most people were by accidents or when they came to die, their chief feeling, surely this can't be happening to *me*.

I saw too that my disbelief could be an attempt to escape, now that the time of my test was coming, and that in the days to come this could become an increasing temptation. I would make myself look at all the people around me who would laugh or be angry if they were told what I knew. I would ask myself, was it possible that they could all be wrong and I alone right. I would argue with myself that even if I was certain I was right, need I commit myself by some irrevocable act; because this might make me less rather than more useful. I would struggle and struggle to escape. Only by standing above my struggles and seeing them clearly as instinctive animal squirmings for self-preservation could I keep myself steady to my duty.

That week we went to dinner with the Quorums.

'Ah ha, the great woodsman,' Charlie Quorum said, standing back with mock ceremonial, keeping that deadpan look on his Victoria-plum face.

One year Jim and Janie Brightworth had given a fancy-dress party and Charlie Quorum had come as a female gypsy pirate. Female and gypsy from his cushiony bosom and big brass earrings, I suppose, and pirate from his baggy trousers and the curved sabre he kept shaking. For several months afterwards I couldn't meet Charlie without feeling that he was missing something – his bosom and sabre, of course. Even now he sometimes seemed to me a disguised female gypsy pirate.

'What's he talking about?' Queenie said to me.

'Don't you know?' Charlie said. 'Lurking in our midst!'

'What, Harry here?' Queenie said, moving back her head, tilting it sideways, giving me a narrow-eyed stare, at the same time holding out both her hands with arms straight so that I had to take them. 'I don't believe it.'

'Isn't a doubt,' Charlie said. 'Caught in the act.'

The conversation made me sweat. I was tempted to have some sudden gripping pain so that I'd have to leave. I forced myself to stay. Apart from not wanting to remind Molly of the incident, I was afraid the Draycotts might come – or be here already, and that times would be mentioned. There was at least an hour of my previous Saturday morning I couldn't account for.

But when I got into the sitting-room it was empty except for Percy Goyle and his peke.

We smiled and shook hands warmly, if rather formally, as Percy seemed to make one. I was so pleased and relieved to see him that for a moment I could not believe it would be hard to talk to him. I even thought of mentioning butterflies, a subject I'd avoided since those early days.

I said the garden was badly dried up.

'Is that so,' Percy said. I recognized the way he often came to a subject I started from a long way away, as if adjusting himself to the strange fact that it interested me, as if this was the thing of interest. Now, when I caught him watching me, he glanced out of the window, as if to help him to understand by actually seeing some dried-up garden. He clearly hadn't noticed and I remembered that he had a gardener.

'Will it affect your . . .' he began and checked himself, either forgetting what I grew or realizing how painful it might be to me.

'Fruit,' I said, to help him. 'I doubt it. I'm lucky.'

At this moment Charlie brought Molly down from the bathroom.

'Ah ha,' he said to Percy. 'Meeting our great ranger of the forests?'

Percy Goyle smiled at him and then began, without hurry, to look round the room for some other guest he hadn't noticed.

'No, no, it's a joke,' I said. Somehow I had to stop this.

'It's not a joke,' Charlie said. In mock anger he crossed to the whisky table. 'It's no joke at all.'

Seeing him pouring whisky reminded me of the time when he'd come to supper and I'd given him my own brand, which I got wholesale from the co-operative that sold me fertilizers and sprays. Presently I'd seen that he hadn't drunk any, which was unusual. Queenie had seen long before.

'Oh Charlie, don't be silly, go home and get it. Harry won't mind.' So he'd gone home and got his own bottle.

Of course I'd laughed. I'd seen that it wasn't another of Charlie's affectations but a genuine taste which genuinely embarrassed him. For about a year after that, each time we'd met he'd apologized, usually starting, 'Look, old chap, your charming reception, I'm terribly sorry, but I honestly find it gives me such a headache, that weed-killer of yours – whatever am I saying . . .'

For the first time I wondered whether I'd fully understood the incident. Why had Charlie been so suspicious of my whisky?

But as the evening continued it was for other reasons that I found my attitude to Charles Quorum changing. And principal of these was the way he went on about the camp-bed incident. I was relieved when dinner started and I knew the Draycotts weren't coming, though as we ate I became afraid they might drop in for coffee and Charlie might still be pursuing this boring joke. I could see that it had become boring not only to me but to everyone else. I wondered why Charlie went on in this untypically boring way . . . About Charlie I had no sudden revelation. I couldn't tell you at what moment that evening I realized.

I sat next to Queenie. Queenie had that special manner which made me believe her when she said her background was 'theatre'. I guessed that long ago she'd had a holiday job looking after the properties for her local rep, of which her mother had been a patron. Whatever it was, she'd decided the manner suited her and never let it go.

'Coming from theatre,' she'd say, as if it was another country. 'Of course that was before I met *him*.' People think when they abuse each other in that sort of playful way no one will guess that they've let real feeling into it. They're wrong. Queenie's real feeling about Charlie showed clearly, and it was love. She abused him because she knew he expected it but with shame, and when she laughed she hoped he'd join.

As Queenie talked to me she often stared at me with big eyes, laying a hand on my wrist and bending forward to force me to look up from the vegetables I was gathering. But occasionally she spoke through closed teeth, her half-closed eyes deliberately focused on a distant wall. Though it was her dinner-party she could talk to me because she didn't serve it. She sat upright, one hand on each side of her plate, and told Charlie what to serve.

'Look at him,' she said in a stage whisper as Charlie carried round the dishes. They were heavy and antique. 'Isn't he nice?' It still surprised her. 'You'd never think he once had three Turks to press his trousers.'

'Charlie's birds,' she said, noticing my fixed stare at the two silver-plated grouse. 'Isn't he *too* bourgeois.' But I saw how they shone and knew who polished them.

As I talked to her about azaleas – like Molly, she loved gardening – I reasoned it out this way: he was a retired First Secretary, the least suspect sort of person. That was a highly suspicious point. A principle I work on when I want to find something is to look twice in the most likely place. When I've looked twice and not found it I look a third time.

'Mine have scarcely a leaf between them,' Queenie said.

'Nor mine,' I said, allowing a hint of her tragic tone to infect my voice.

Next point, he'd come to this part of the country for no obvious reason – no childhood associations, no old school or service friends. At least twice I'd heard him mention how he'd chanced to see the house advertised on the noticeboard of a Chelsea newsagent among models and corduroy fetishists – as an illustration of how good can come of evil. That was a strange subject to have occurred spontaneously twice in the times we'd been here.

'Or do they anyway lose their leaves when they've bloomed?' I asked.

'They certainly don't,' Queenie said, drawing herself up.

Then, what a huge house it was for a childless retired pair in their early sixties, and how little of the inside we'd ever been shown.

'You could try watering them,' I said.

'Do you think he would?' she asked, taking my upper arm in both her hands, bending her cheek close to mine, turning her eyes towards Charlie.

Again, there were his long solitary rounds of golf. What better opportunity for contact work?

'But wouldn't it make their little roots turn up?' Queenie said, looking into my eyes, tense for my answer. 'Expecting more, and it never coming?'

'Maybe,' I said. I was following the golf idea, remembering how Queenie had once told me that although he was retired he still went a solitary early morning round on Saturdays. 'So he can be lazy for the rest of the week-end,' she'd said. 'But' – gripping me and whispering loudly so that he'd hear – 'I think it's because he hasn't noticed he's retired.'

And if he hadn't noticed he'd retired, why was that? Because he didn't feel retired? Because he was still at work?

No doubt it was risky, but towards the end of dinner I had what I thought a clever idea. Turning to Queenie, who was stage-whispering to Percy on her other side – I could see him leaning away as if she were frightening him – I said, 'The trouble with this weather is the way it makes the milk go bad.'

At that moment there was complete silence in everyone's conversation. Queenie stopped talking to Percy. I could understand that, because out of context my remark may have seemed odd.

More important, Charlie stopped talking to Molly, as he had been, about the way the seats of his Citroën let down to make a double bed. I was sure he'd had more to say about that.

Pretending to be totally unaware of this I went on, 'It means you must only order one or at most two pints at a time.'

'Oh, I can't see why,' Queenie said.

'But it makes such lovely cheese,' Molly said.

Percy was bright red and feeding himself fast with teaspoonfuls of fruit salad, in embarrassed sympathy for me, I guessed.

'Now out in the wilds . . .' Charlie began, but he didn't go on and no one laughed.

When dinner was over I had a chance I'd been waiting for. I strolled out through the french windows into the garden. I walked away from the house between lawns with sprinklers and herbaceous borders giving off heavy scents in the falling dusk.

Their garden was like a deep tropical channel. On either side beyond the lawns and the herbaceous borders vast banks of rhododendrons rose fifteen or twenty feet, hiding everything beyond except occasional pine tops. They made the garden seem part of some huge forest. Though it was probably not much bigger than its neighbours, I never imagined it having boundaries.

Except at the bottom, of course, where I now hurried and where the rhododendrons closed in and a pathway led under them. Beyond this there was peaty ground free of undergrowth below tall trees. A single wire on slim posts, several of which were missing, made a doubtful boundary with the common. It could have been crossed at a dozen places by scarcely lifting a foot. Moreover the dry needles underfoot would have left little sign if there had been a path to a regular crossing place.

I hurried away. Already I'd been too long. Just before I passed again under the rhododendrons I stopped and looked back between the pine trunks. I don't know what I thought I'd learn. I'd already located the pale shape of the Draycotts' house across a short stretch of common, even shorter than I'd expected. I'd already been surprised to see how little back garden it had, perhaps seven yards, as if Rene Draycott's father had suddenly become impatient at the idea that he should give them a back garden too. Now, as I looked towards that stunted piece of ground, I saw a movement. There was someone in a pale shirt standing by the garden fence.

Had he been there all the time, unnoticed in the dusk till he moved? Or had he just come out? If he'd just come out, why had he chosen this moment? If he'd seen me, had it been possible for him to see who I was? What was that strange object he seemed to be waving over his head, like a saw? These and other questions raced through my mind as I hurried back up that deep garden like a tropical valley. The dark banks of rhododendrons seemed to look down on it and made me want to run.

I didn't enjoy the rest of the evening. Again I needed quiet to think. I couldn't respond cheerily when Jim Brightworth, who came with Janie for coffee, slapped me on the shoulder. 'What's this I hear?' he shouted. 'Taking to the fields?'

'Charlie's imagination . . .' I said.

'Last seen disappearing over the horizon with two sticks.'

'A camp-bed,' I said. 'Which I was offering to a friend.'

'Can't get out of it that way,' Jim shouted.

'Be quiet, you noisy brute,' Janie said.

'How's the pool?' I said.

'You see, he's changing the subject,' Jim shouted, though less loudly.

'He's been looking for a site in our garden,' Queenie giggled.

It was hard for me to control my anger that they had noticed, anger not with Queenie but with Charlie who, I knew, had been the one who'd seen me go.

At that moment all the things I'd liked about him became the reasons for my hating him. His perpetual heavy humour which, I saw, far from giving conversation interest concentrated it on the single boring question of what Charlie was hinting. I saw this perpetual comic mysteriousness not only as offensive in itself, but as a clever technique of concealment.

But I forced myself to smile, knowing that nothing of this must show.

It meant of course qualifying my theory about the Draycotts – so I thought at the time. I could do that. Compared to Wilfred Draycott, Charlie Quorum seemed infinitely sinister.

I was pleased to notice, glancing sideways, that Molly and Percy Goyle weren't joining the joke, as if they might not have understood it. They were near the window, having the same careful but often silent conversation I'd noticed them having at the Brightworths' barbecue. It was as if Molly had discovered a way of communicating with Percy and they both understood this.

I was also pleased when Mrs. Willis came, unexpectedly late, for coffee. Perhaps she could fit it in before her bridge. She seemed older that night, with deeper powder-filled crevices, though just as blue-rinsed. I liked her. I liked the way she went on defiantly enjoying herself at an age when dying must seem close, when she must more and more be doing it for herself as other people's opinions became less and less important.

The moon, which was in its last quarter, hadn't risen when we went home, so that although the sky was clear and full of stars the drive was dark and we missed the entrance. Molly took my arm. I didn't see our house till it loomed above us.

Lying in bed beside her, though not touching her, I couldn't sleep. Perhaps it was the black coffee; or the way I was remembering all that had happened that evening, trying to understand it, remembering an increasing number of Charlie's Irish eccentricities which I must now reassess. I felt Molly turn over several times before she seemed to grow quiet.

'Harry,' she said.

I jumped, hearing her speak suddenly out of the darkness when I'd thought she was asleep. I realized that she'd been lying on her back, wide awake.

'Uh huh,' I said, making it more sleepy than I was.

'Are things all right?'

It frightened me. I was glad not to answer for several seconds, taking cover under my pretended sleepiness. What did she mean? What had she noticed? I thought of asking whether she'd smelt fire or heard a burglar. But if she was really suspicious I must not offer her such chances of hiding it again.

'Aren't they?' I said. I half turned on to my back, as if waking to listen.

After several seconds she said, 'I don't know,' and sighed.

I moved across the bed and put an arm across her chest and my head against her shoulder. She didn't move.

'Tell me,' I said.

'We don't quarrel any more,' she said.

It was more disturbing than I'd expected. The moment she said it I knew she was right.

'Don't we?' I was too surprised to think of anything better. 'That's good then.' It was what I should have said at once.

She didn't answer, just lay still. I had the odd idea that she might cry.

I began to stroke her and kiss her shoulder where her nightdress didn't cover it. At first she wouldn't move, then she turned her back and wriggled close.

Of course we'd quarrelled, though it had been something Molly didn't enjoy. I had sometimes realized that it was the way she never got the spirit of a quarrel but always seemed to be made unhappy by it that annoyed me. Even that doesn't quite explain the shocked, almost dizzy feeling I'd sensed in her when I'd occasionally been angry with her.

It was her complete lack of a sense of time that had occasionally made me shout at her. I'd seen her become quiet and honestly try to hurry. I'd seen how this was muddling her and making her slower.

What a fool I'd been, not to notice that it hadn't happened lately. Still worse, it was too late to invent quarrels. I'm a good actor, but not that good. Every quarrelsome thing I'd have said I'd have seen her guessing why I was saying it.

I didn't sleep much that night. It was the first of many when I could only sleep for a few hours before dawn.

I held Molly and my arm became numb and then got pins and needles. I moved it carefully but still lay close to her. From her even breathing I thought she was asleep.

During the hours I lay awake I decided what I must do.

Saturday dawned fine and clear and I slipped out of bed at five without waking Molly. She wouldn't think that odd. I stood in the veranda, not showing myself, looking down across my orchards to the golf course. It was still in shadow. Its sandy bunkers and neat clumps of bushes and smooth fairways reminded me of the sand table we'd had at school for teaching military tactics. I'd always hoped we'd use it but we never did.

My plan was to wait till I saw Charlie Quorum drive down the New Lane, then to hurry down the hillside, through my orchards, and reach my side of the golf course not much later than he would reach the first tee. My fear was that 'early' to Charlie might mean around eight o'clock by which time Molly and the children would be about.

I'd thought of taking my Mauser. That was a beautiful gun, with a magazine to hold ten and a wooden holster to fix to the grip to make a shoulder butt. Like that it could be fired accurately up to two hundred metres. It was typically German, but with the flavour of a pre-First War Germany of archdukes and junkers. It was the sort of piece of industrial design that lasts fifty years beyond its time, a Rolls Royce of automatic pistols – and it was about as handy as a Rolls Royce.

No, for a gun which wouldn't keep catching round my ankles I'd have chosen my Beretta. That was a beautiful gun too, but in an Italian way. It was beautifully neat to look at. Its three-and-a-half-inch barrel could be replaced in a couple of seconds when it got red-hot from rapid fire. I didn't take it because I didn't trust it to shoot straight at *two* metres, let alone golf course ranges.

It was still so early – before five-thirty – that I allowed myself to stroll along the drive towards my front gate. Small birds were hopping on the gravel and fluttering in the bushes. A blackbird made a low approach over some shrubs and landed five yards from me, cocking its tail. I suppose he was in the habit of behaving so carelessly at such an hour in the morning. A second later he'd seen me and taken off with a high warning cackle. I wondered if Charlie might also behave carelessly in the early morning. At that moment, long before I'd expected, I heard a rushing of wheels and his yellow Citroën hurried past.

There had been no time to take cover and I watched foolishly. I could only hope that because our drive met the New Lane at an angle he hadn't seen me. I thought I would have noticed if he had looked over his shoulder, as he would have had to. What I couldn't tell was whether he'd glanced in his mirror.

There wasn't a moment to lose and I bounded down the hillside. I went close to the chestnut palings which separated my ground from Percy Goyle's, aiming for the point where my orchards bordered with the golf course. I'd forgotten how steep it was. Several times my feet slid away and I only held myself by beech saplings; and once I tripped forward on to my knees in some heather, bruising one on a hidden stone. I was wet with sweat and limping by the time I reached the gap in the hedge I'd marked. It had taken longer than I expected. Charlie had already driven off and was coming towards me not a hundred yards away in the direction of the first green.

I won't describe his whole round. There are only a few important points. Mostly he plodded after his shots in a determined but entirely conventional way, as if he might still be half asleep. In the open country I noticed his nautical roll. He moved his legs as if they were separate, trunk-like objects which he was placing one at a time in front of him, and his body swayed above them.

He was wearing a new beige wind-jacket. It was so new that it didn't fit him properly. He wore it like a naughty schoolboy who has been put into it by his mother but won't try to make it fit. It was zipped up to the chin but the collar point of a tartan shirt stuck up half-way along one side of his red neck.

I didn't try to follow him closely. There wasn't enough cover. But I'd planned my positions so that I'd be close to him at several points in the first nine holes. He wasn't likely to play more. In particular there was a long, well-bushed ridge which was near the fourth tee at one end and the fifth tee at the other. I could reach this ridge across some low ground which would be out of sight while he was playing the third. Unfortunately there was no corresponding out-of-sight period after the fifth before the sixth took him right along the side of my ridge. If he made a bad shot and came up there to hunt for his ball he might stumble on me before I had had any chance to escape.

It was a chance I had to take. I got there safely as I'd planned and was only about five yards from him when he drove off for the fourth. I heard him grunt at the same instant that I heard his driver whack the ball, an involuntary grunt of air forced out by the effort. After that he took a pace forward and stood watching it, hand raised above his eyes. He was humming, I noticed, on an ascending note as his ball soared, then a descending note as it fell. He ended with a dramatic suddenness that told as plainly as if I'd seen it that he'd landed in a bunker. His timing was perfect and I had to check my laugh which even when alone he had played for.

He must have done that hole quickly because I'd only just traversed the ridge to my position near the fifth tee when I heard him panting up to it. It wasn't a good position, because it gave me only a narrow view of him through a gorse bush, but it had the advantage that it was so close that I could hear every noise his clothes made as he bent and stamped around. And it was well hidden: the gorse bush was one of the thickest and I was at its centre. Unfortunately the ground below a gorse bush is an uncomfortable place to kneel and I had had no time to clear it. Apart from the live spikes which were against my face and arms I could feel a dead one going deeply into my left and already bruised knee.

Perhaps it was this which distracted me, because a second later I had no idea what had taken him out of my sight. He was still extremely close, even closer than before, judging by his puffing. I didn't dare turn my head an inch.

But I went on trying to guess why, when he had already teed up his ball, he had moved towards the bushes. Had he dropped another ball which had run in this direction and he was now fetching? Or seen a nice piece of gorse for a buttonhole? More alarming, had he noticed something strange in the gorse bush, which he was now staring down on, with raised club, or was he ready to burst into heavy laughter?

As I listened, my skull creeping at the idea of the blow which might be hanging over it, I heard the most astonishing noise. It was a sort of squelching hiss. I didn't begin to recognize it. Perhaps I would never have recognized it if, a few seconds later when I could see him again by the tee, I hadn't noticed Charlie give his nose a single upward wipe on the sleeve of his new beige wind-jacket. At once I had no doubt: Charlie Quorum had been blowing his nose into the bushes.

I've always found this a peculiarly disgusting habit. When I thought of Charlie doing it, his finger and thumb compressing that spot-holed nose, the hanging trails of snot he'd had to lodge on the bushes, I wanted to come out and strike him. It was an impulse which frightened me because there was a second when I didn't care how disastrous it would be.

I forced myself to try to guess what it might mean. As soon as I began to reason I felt calmer.

I saw at once that there might be nothing to explain: Charlie had failed to put a handkerchief in his new jacket pocket. His nose had started to run. It didn't remove my surprise that an ex-First Secretary should do such a thing, even when he was of Irish extraction and believed himself alone. He would have to overcome years of habit training. And he had done it on the open end of a ridge where he was in silhouette for several hundred yards in three directions.

I'd got no farther than this – it had taken me only a second and Charlie still hadn't driven – when something even more interesting began to happen. I heard a shout. Directly beyond Charlie, still a hundred yards from him in the direction of the club house, I saw a figure advancing down the fairway.

He came closer. He shouted again, 'Hallo there.' He was unusually tall. I became increasingly sure that it was Jim Brightworth.

Presently I could see his big pointed nose. He carried a bag of clubs slung on his shoulder and was wearing the sort of narrow cap with a peak that American generals wear for golf. The peak of his cap was a similar shape and about as long as his nose.

'I made it,' Jim shouted.

He came up to the tee and watched Charlie drive.

I'd expected something, of course, or I wouldn't have been here. Jim was the last thing I'd expected. It made me realize that I'd half expected Wilfred Draycott. All my tentative theories of the last three days now had to be reshaped.

Either I was mistaken and Charlie's early-morning golf was the genuine health-obsession of a retired man; or more sinister and complicated things were happening around me than I'd imagined.

Perhaps it was strange that I should start to discover these now, and never have seen them before, despite the careful way I had watched. There were two explanations: first, I might have watched in the wrong way, or without the conviction that there was anything to discover; second, perhaps there *had been* nothing to discover. I had a sense of some crisis at hand which was disturbing them into this new and almost panicky activity. It fitted with the alert I'd had.

When he'd teed up Jim flexed his arms, pretended to roll up his sleeves, shouted 'fore' down the empty fairway and drove. If they said anything else to each other they did it too cleverly for me to hear.

'That'll make you smile on the other side of your arse,' Jim shouted. Charlie gave some poker-faced grunts, and they went away in diverging directions in pursuit of their balls.

The next twenty minutes were alarming. If Charlie had been alone I might have risked a dash across the open when his back was turned. To trust that both of them would stay facing away for long enough for me to reach my orchard was absurd. Anyway the risk of waiting now seemed worthwhile. It wasn't likely that they would talk at such an obvious place as a tee, where recording microphones could be fixed. If they spoke to each other it would be in open country.

I spent those minutes making ground along the ridge. I did it in short rushes for I was in full view. Every few yards I dropped like a shot animal and lay flat till I was sure I'd not been seen. I stopped when I found a dense bush.

I got deeply into it. I took a double handful of peaty soil and wiped my face with it. I stuck some twigs in my hair. By the time I saw them turn towards the sixth tee I felt safe – unless a ball actually trickled up to me, and even then I might trickle it away. Or unless one of them lost a ball and began to beat about.

An advantage I had, even if they passed close, was that the sun had risen and was lighting the course brightly, but it was still so low that it cast the long black shadow of my ridge half across their fairway. Glancing from there towards me they would be dazzled.

I was relieved when they each made straight shots and advanced in similar directions, Charlie twenty yards ahead. As soon as Jim found his ball he gave an enormous laugh. He stood looking at it. He gave another. 'Well, bugger me,' he shouted. Charlie seemed not to hear till he had hit his own, then came across.

They stood together looking at it and I could see Charlie's chest bouncing with intentionally unhidden hidden laughter. When Jim played there was an all round spatter of earth as if a small explosive shell had hit the ground. They went off together.

Ten minutes later I was doubling along my orchard fence, climbing the hillside to my garden. I reached the bathroom unseen and washed.

That day we went for a picnic. To my family's surprise I drove ten miles to reach the coast road. I told them I had an idea – that was true.

I joined the Saturday creep to that hillside which we could see from our house. Towards the summit, before it doubled back and went over the top, there were several side tracks down which cars could turn on to heath land. Some were already occupied by parties with aluminium folding chairs and gas-cylinder stoves.

I went a few yards down one which looked difficult and seemed less used – but there were others it might have been. Anyway, I wasn't sure what I hoped to discover.

I got out the glasses and helped Dan and Peggy find our house. It wasn't easy. Even when I had the line of them, ours seemed curiously unlike itself, lower and pinker and half hidden at one end by what must have been my fir copse. Oddly, the most prominent and recognizable was Percy Goyle's neo-Tudor mansion. Its double row of twirled Tudor chimneys were plain and so was the circle of his lawn among trees, as if it must have been tilted in this direction. Close to the veranda was a small mark which might have been Percy himself sitting in a deckchair reading, as he often did.

We drove on. We ate cold chicken and drank cider. We lay in the dappled shade – it was too hot in the sun – and Dan and Peggy climbed trees. They were unexpectedly quiet and I knew what was going to happen about a second before the first twig hit my shirt.

It should have been pleasant by that peaceful wood. I should have felt calmed after the two hours we'd spent in engine fumes, advancing and halting, blocked by things ahead we couldn't see. Gradually I should have been able to forget that they were all around me, filling the roads, and lose the sense that I could still hear their engines. I was too worried.

I was worried that I'd left home, putting myself out of touch at such a time. But perhaps I was more worried by the ideas that Jim Brightworth was someone different from the person I'd thought him. I tried to fit deceit behind his schoolboy warmth. I tried to fit a deeper cunning behind his schoolboy motives, which always seemed most transparent when he tried to hide them. I couldn't do it.

It was dangerous to become over-observant, reading significance into the insignificant. A casual round of golf by friends who were not such close friends of mine that I knew their every movement. Was I becoming jumpy?

I drove home. I mowed the lawn. There was work to do in the orchards but I preferred to stay near the house.

The message about the escape procedure came that evening. Somehow the fact that I'd been half expecting it all day made it more, not less of a shock. It was a shock to realize that I didn't take the escape procedure seriously.

I was on the tennis court where Dan and Peggy had called me to show me their game. They'd got the idea from something I'd said that long rallies were the test of ability and were concentrating on these to the exclusion of trying to win points. They'd given up scoring and were counting rally shots, till at twenty-seven Peggy missed because she could no longer wait to hear how impressed I'd been. It was a record. She stood in front of me wanting, I thought, to be hugged, while Dan at the other end shouted, 'You little wet'. At that moment I heard the telephone.

I began to run away from them across the lawn towards the house with what must have seemed surprising abruptness. Normally I'm calm about telephone calls.

All the way I could hear it ringing. I heard not only the soft bell in the office but the loud one outside the back door clanging towards the fir trees. They didn't seem exactly synchronized. I wanted to get there before Molly. If she'd been indoors she'd have reached it already, so I knew she was somewhere in the garden but couldn't remember where, and as I ran I glanced left and right for the wheelbarrow or garden tools but didn't see them. I pushed past the office chair and lifted the receiver. I heard the dialling tone.

It had been ringing up to the moment I lifted it. At exactly the same second they must have put down their receiver. That was the first thought I had.

I worked the receiver rest up and down in quick flashes, giving the ready-to-receive signal. Still nothing happened. I don't know why I went on listening. Presently I could hear them.

What was clever was that the dialling tone wasn't interrupted by their voice. It went on all the time and the voice was behind it, not much louder but perfectly distinct. I guessed what it meant. They'd tapped the wire.

It gave me the feeling that they were near again, a feeling I hadn't had since that first message, typed in my office. And even then I'd felt they'd come and gone. Those three men flashing to me across the country had emphasized my sense of isolation. That was as near as they could get, because things which I couldn't even guess at were going wrong. It was why I'd driven out there on the way to our picnic. Now I felt that we were winning again. They were operating close around me and I was one of them. It was a comforting feeling. Later I lost it.

Speaking through the dialling tone they gave me the instructions, starting with destruction of secret material, going on to disposal of weapons and ending with procedure at rendezvous. Where this would be and how I was to get there I would be told at the time. Meanwhile there were the code words to memorize and the change of clothes to prepare.

I listened carefully, making a few notes. Suddenly it didn't seem to matter that neither I nor they should take the escape procedure seriously. It had to be arranged. That was all.

At first as I listened I said 'yes,' but after a time I stopped because it made it harder to hear what they were saying. Also they didn't pause for my answers and I began to guess that they might not be able to hear me. I was sure of this when they ended, 'Acknowledge by field signal'.

I put down the receiver and came out of the office. Molly was in the kitchen. She must have come from the garden while I'd been phoning. If she'd been in the kitchen before, she would surely have answered it.

PART FOUR

Acknowledge by field signal. Suddenly one more thing made sense.

That bright red helicopter we saw every few days, making its rather aimless progress across the sky, as if as much interested in the ground as in getting anywhere. Or perhaps I was imagining things. There was no need for the whole machine to be ours. More likely a single member of the crew, who could do what was needed, without disclosing himself.

I was worried about the word 'field'. It would have been easier to use the tennis court. There was no way for other people to look down on that. My orchards were entirely overlooked from the house and there was a chance that Molly – or more likely Peggy – might ask what it meant.

I could explain the crates but I wouldn't know what to say about their pattern. She might then wonder why I was getting out the crates at all, on a Sunday, doing it myself without Grant, who helps me with the spraying and other jobs. There was a moment when such questions became self-increasing, like a fire which takes hold and begins to look for new things to burn, unlike the individual sticks which are always ready to smoulder out. They were the sort of questions I must never let start.

But the crates seemed the only possible way. Looking down from the front drive after breakfast, I picked a place which was partly hidden by trees from here but would probably be clear from above. It was fifty yards from the sheds.

Getting them out and carrying them that distance took me most of the morning. I was glad to have the work. I'd got them about half arranged. I was halfway between the shape I was making and the shed, carrying one under each arm, when I suddenly stopped. I'd had a picture of myself as if from above. Though I was hot and sweating it made me cold all over. My knees felt shaky. My arms felt weak and I thought I might drop the crates. There I was, small and busy. There was that curious half-formed hieroglyphic. What on earth was I doing?

I wanted to pause and think but I knew that I mustn't. I turned and began to stumble with my crates back to the shed. I left them there and hurried back to that signal which I had imagined I was making. The sight of it horrified me. I began to run round it, pushing the crates right and left out of shape. I put them into other arbitrary groups here and there under the trees. Anything to destroy that awful mad sign. I stood still in the full sun, shivering violently like a man with a fever.

Near me two remained together. They had formed the base of the shape's first upright stroke. I put a third next to them, then a fourth and a fifth. I lifted it and threw it ten yards into the trees. I threw them all violently away. When I missed my grip on one I kicked it and my foot splintered the wood and became caught inside. I beat it against a tree trunk, breaking it into pieces and taking a long graze of skin from my shin.

I stood looking round me at the confusion I had made. Crates and bits of broken wood lay everywhere. What did it mean?

Now I could start to put them away. Now I could go up the hillside back to my home I liked and my wife and children I loved. I was better now. And when that red helicopter came presently, buzzing and hovering, it would see no sign. I went on my knees in the dry grass and held my hair in my hands, pulling at its roots. If only I knew. If only I knew.

Presently I knew that it was a risk I couldn't take. Slowly and painfully, limping from my hurt shin, I rearranged the crates. I fetched others from the shed and completed the shape.

I fetched nails and a hammer and began to repair the broken ones. I listened all the time and sometimes looked up into the blue sky with its puffs of fair weather cumulus.

I listened all afternoon.

Towards evening I became anxious. There was a limit to the time I could leave them there in that 'message understood' symbol. Even if I risked it for the night, Grant was coming in the morning and would start to move them as he worked on them. I would have no reason for stopping him.

We began supper. Outside it was still warm though less stifling than the afternoon. The morning clouds, instead of growing to thunder size, as I had expected, had gone away. The sunlight had turned yellow and the long shadows of the pines were on the lawn. Here in the kitchen I noticed a beam turning the black foot-plate of the hot-water boiler grey. I was watching this with surprise that it should have penetrated to this unexpected corner when I heard it.

I heard it long before the others. It was loud before they heard it. It seemed to come directly over the house, and lower than I remembered so that it stopped our talking.

When it was gone Molly said, 'What are you smiling at?'

It was true, a foolish smile had come on my face. 'The noise,' I said. 'The way we couldn't hear ourselves think.' I went on smiling and frowning.

That Monday I found the footprint.

I'd just come down from my attic to cross off the day on my calendar – there were eleven left. I'd come out of the office on to the sunny lawn to check Wilfred Draycott and Jim Brightworth leaving for the station. Wilfred's mini approached with a hurried whine which faded quickly as soon as he reached the New Lane because his drive joined it below ours. Jim's Jaguar went into the dip below our lawn with a plushy roar, less like an engine than a furnace breathing. And I'd gone from this sunny side of the house to the shade at the back. I saw it in a small flower-bed.

No part of this bed was fertile and the inner two feet which were always in shade and sheltered from the rain by the house eaves were completely bare. A thin crust had formed on them. At the centre of this bare inner margin, crushing the crust into the soft soil below, was a distinct footprint.

It was recent, that was the first thing I saw. The inch of discoloured undersoil round its edge looked fresh. Anyway I would have noticed it. At least once a day I made the circuit of the house by that back way which connected my two drives. And I kept my eyes open. True, I had been preoccupied the day before but I remembered coming here at tea-time while I was listening for the helicopter. That left the evening and the night.

Next, it was a left shoe, and I could tell which way they had been going. But there wasn't a window or drain pipe for eight feet in either direction.

The apparent pointlessness of it disturbed me. Not only was there no way up or into the house which they could have been surveying but they couldn't have been crossing from one place to another because the flower-bed occupied a triangular corner where the kitchen stuck out backwards from the rest of the house. I felt this should be the clue to the problem and worried over it. An added complication was that the footprint was set parallel to the house wall so that the fetching something theory – a ball or paper aeroplane – wouldn't work. And there had been about equal weight on the toe and heel so that it wasn't a halting mark.

I know as well as anyone that you don't get a single footprint. Montbretia grew in a reedy mat close to the sheltered margin of arid soil and I bent and examined it for another, but it seemed everywhere equally crushed.

After that came the shoe size, a vital point. Here I had to be careful because the way it had sunk into the soil made it look bigger than it was. To get a better view I stepped from the drive on to the eighteen-inch stone wall which contained the bed and leant forward, peering closely. Too big for my children, I thought, but small for a man. Man's size five and a half, I guessed. As I bent I half-toppled and had to stand quickly, circling my arms backwards to keep my balance on the wall. It was then that I saw Molly about twenty yards away, standing quite still, watching me. She was in the drive immediately outside our front door, and unlike me she was in the sun. I could see the sunlight in her fair hair.

'What *are* you doing?' she called.

'Working things out,' I said with quiet confidence.

I came down from the wall and moved towards her, but backwards, looking now at the house roof, now at the flower-bed.

'The gutters,' I said, preoccupied, still not turning to her.

'What's wrong with them?'

'We're going to make our fortune.' After more pause I turned to her. 'A mirror device to tell you if your gutters are full of leaves without hiring a fifty-foot ladder.'

She laughed and turned away. It had been a near thing.

All that sunny morning, as I worked with Grant on the crates, I thought about the footprint. At twelve I came up to the house, and soon afterwards, when I heard Molly take the car to go shopping, I went to look at it again. With me I took one of her left shoes from the lobby.

Treading carefully on the flattened montbretia so that I wouldn't leave a mark or disturb any I still might find, I moved on to the flower-bed. I squatted and leant forward holding the shoe in both hands. I lowered it carefully, arms outstretched. I heard a high voice call 'Daddee'.

I stood and began to move back fast. I'd only taken two steps when I heard it much louder and half the distance away. I was recovering my balance from jumping clear of the bed when I saw her in the drive, exactly where Molly had stood early that morning.

'Daddy, when was William the First born?'

She went on coming towards me but more slowly. She was close to tears, though she kept them back better than she would have done the holidays before. I thought there'd been a fight.

'Born?' I said, making time. 'You mean actually born?'

'Dan says . . .' she began. Then she'd seen it. 'Daddy, what's that?'

'If you mean when did he become king . . .' I said.

'Daddy, why have you got one of Mummy's shoes?'

'Oh that,' I said, bringing it casually from behind my back, still too preoccupied to attend properly. 'You see, he must have become king of Normandy first, that's a funny thought.'

'What is?' She glanced quickly behind her. 'What's funny?' She stopped about two yards away, looking up at me. 'Daddy, why have you got one of Mummy's shoes?'

'She lost it,' I said, definitely annoyed this time. 'You see, the date we all know is 1066. What was Dan asking?'

At that moment Molly came round the end of the house.

Usually I heard the car. She might have brought it up the back drive and put it straight into the garage. Or she might have parked it on the front drive. Whichever she'd done, I'd have expected to hear it. I must have been distracted.

It did flash through my mind that I couldn't remember hearing it go out. I knew I must have heard it because otherwise I wouldn't have known she was shopping, but I couldn't actually bring back the sound as a recent memory.

'Home already?' I said.

'Mummy, Daddy's found the shoe you lost.'

'Me?' she said vaguely.

'That didn't take long,' I said.

'Mummy, Daddy's found your shoe.'

There seemed no choice so I handed it to her. 'Rescued from the dog,' I said.

Dan came round the corner of the house singing, 'Who didn't know, ten sixty-six, who didn't know, ten sixty-six.'

'But we haven't got a dog,' Molly said. She seemed genuinely confused.

I just grinned enigmatically.

'Where did you find it?'

Dan stopped singing. 'Who?' he said, sensing mystery. 'What?'

'Back there.' I gestured with a thumb, and sauntered past them as if no longer interested.

Behind me I could hear Peggy explaining with impatient condescension to Dan, 'Daddy says he rescued Mummy's shoe from the dog, but Mummy says we haven't got a dog.' She had a way of clearing things to their essentials.

Molly didn't say anything.

'I think Daddy's the dog,' Peggy said. It gave me a shock, making me halt, then stroll on. I hoped they hadn't noticed.

All the same I thought I'd acted quickly and well – till late that evening when I happened to pass up the back drive behind the house and glance at that triangular flower-bed in the angle. Its inner margin was perfectly smooth.

There wasn't a mark. The only change was that its thin soil crust had gone. Completely gone. The whole inner two feet were smooth soft brown. I didn't pause as I strolled casually past.

That week I sold the fruit crop on the trees. There wasn't any choice.

It was something I hadn't done in other years, though pickers had been a growing problem. In our part of the country, becoming more a commuters' suburb all the time, they had been harder each year to find, even when you offered absurd wages. I'd gone on trying because, anxious as it made me, I'd enjoyed picking time.

I'd enjoyed the starts at dawn when the fruit was still cold and our fingers grew numb. And the numbness of mind when we'd been doing it for sixteen hours, almost without a break – that was a strange feeling, and one I didn't know any other way of reaching. It had put me beyond the ordinary things I worried about. Suddenly, around supper-time, I'd find I no longer wanted it to be finished so that I could rest my aching arms and shoulders. I wasn't anxious any more about how much we'd done that day and whether a gale would come before we'd finished. These problems were still there but they'd receded in importance. It was easy any day to make them recede by looking at them from a hundred years or another star. This was different. I wasn't driving them away with a philosophical attack but genuinely felt they weren't important, weren't even real.

Once I remember, long after the pickers had gone, Molly and I had found that we were picking by moonlight. We'd gone on so long into the dusk that the light of the full moon had become more use than the daylight. We'd stopped then, but in spite of our exhaustion we hadn't wanted to.

And when it was over, the boxes being piled on to the lorry and driven away, I'd enjoyed that too, though in a different way.

I think I was most worried that for marketing reasons the contractors might in the end find it uneconomic to pick our crop. Ours might be the marginal one they didn't want. They'd have made their profit elsewhere and ours would be a small contribution to the debit side already allowed for. They'd be under no obligation to increase their loss. Molly wouldn't see it that way. The fruit rotting on our trees would upset her. She'd want to pick it herself. No one would persuade her that because it had been paid for it had done its job, wasn't even hers to pick.

I made the first phone call on Monday and the deal was fixed on Wednesday. That was the day we gave our tennis party. All my instincts were against it. I wasn't sure if I could be polite.

Without consulting me Molly had asked the Draycotts over for a game. She said she'd done it when she heard he'd begun his holiday. Everything followed from that. The first thing that followed was that Wilfred fell through a cucumber frame. He'd literally been dragged off his feet, Rene said, when exercising Boodles on a lead.

He had to be exercised on a lead because about a mile and a half away there was a bitch in heat and this was making him sex mad. Wilfred had taken him out at dusk and a faint breath of wind must have come from the southeast because the next thing he'd known he was right inside the frame with deep cuts on both hands. The odd thing was, Boodles had been so shocked by what he'd done, he'd stood and gaped.

She hoped we'd excuse Wilfred for not ringing himself, but his hands . . . They'd so looked forward to it. Ever since they'd been asked. Of course we wouldn't want her alone. She hardly bothered to say it. Perhaps it was this that made me insist they should come, when it was exactly the excuse I'd hoped for. 'Of course you must,' I said. 'And bring Wilfred to watch.'

'We'll ask Jim and Janie,' Molly said. 'Jim's just started his holiday.'

It was my shocked surprise at this coincidence which stopped me objecting at once. Then it was too late.

When I rang Jim he said he'd unfortunately arranged something with Charlie Quorum. Golf? I was about to ask. I checked myself, remembering that I didn't know. 'Bring him too,' I said cheerily.

'That's an idea,' Jim said.

I held on to the receiver for several seconds while Jim calculated.

'That's quite an idea,' he said. 'We'll do that.'

'And bring Hubert,' I said.

'Hubert!' Jim said. 'Tennis! You're mad.'

Though I was surprising myself by the way I was extending this casual game with the Draycotts to a party, I'd already begun to realize that it wasn't a mistake. I needed more evidence, needed it badly.

Half an hour before they were due I discovered that Molly had asked Mrs. Willis to drop in for tea.

'May as well be hung for a sheep as a lamb,' she said.

I was startled that she should use this particular cliché. Looking at her, I wondered if she'd startled herself. I had the strange feeling that there was a second when we might have had a wry laugh together.

'I had to ring her about the Michaelmas daisies,' Molly said.

I'd never imagined that Mrs. Willis gardened, and said so.

'I know,' Molly said and paused as if it worried her too. 'Perhaps she wants them for a present.'

'Can they be transplanted at this time of year?'

'That's the trouble,' Molly said, as if she was thinking about something else.

'When it's so dry,' we said simultaneously, stared at each other and broke out laughing. I didn't understand why.

'She must be lonely,' Molly said.

'Mrs. Willis?' I said. 'I thought she was the centre of a gang of septuagenarian bridge-fiends.'

'That's true,' Molly said, but not as if she thought so.

From the start I found that afternoon upsetting. There was a strange atmosphere which, watch and listen as I would, I couldn't attach to anything. One difficulty was that I didn't seem able to listen well. It was an old fear I'd had, that I was going deaf. When I was playing I could see that the others who were standing together watching were saying things, but I couldn't catch them. I could only hear the faintest murmuring, as if from far away. When I was watching I could see the various partners speaking to each other between points or in quick asides during rallies, but the words didn't reach me.

No doubt it was partly the effect of the heat. That afternoon seemed to be the hottest we'd had. It was humid too. Soon after lunch there were tall columns of cloud and in the distance several heavy rolls of thunder. They were some way off but I thought they'd be coming closer.

First to arrive were the Draycotts. Rene was in white shorts, white socks and white tunic. In this costume she looked more than usually like a mousey schoolgirl. Wilfred had both hands in bandages, one arm in a sling and a piece of plaster on the side of his nose.

How had he got his nose into it?

As we weren't yet enough to play we listened while they made apologies. They seemed to drive each other on, falling into a competition of self-humiliation. As if they sensed something, they came to a faltering halt.

'It just would happen yesterday,' Rene said.

I braced myself to interpose a new subject, however rudely, but already they were telling us that as well as our tennis invitation (if anything could be as well as that) Rene's parents had been coming next day. Could you beat it? It was as if unless Wilfred had both hands in full use he did not trust himself to show sufficient gratitude.

The Quorums came next. Charlie wore white flannels tied up by a mauve handkerchief. Though big, this was so stretched by his belly that its corners could only meet in a tiny knot in front. His belly didn't sag but stuck out solidly below his ribs with the curved shape of a squat gas cylinder.

'I'll have you,' Charlie began.

'He means for damages, dear,' Queenie explained.

She wore a white pleated skirt above her knees, which were mottled, and a tight vest of horizontal orange and white stripes. She wore several golden bracelets on each of her big sandy arms, which were bare to the shoulder. Though dressed to play, she later refused and I guessed she hadn't meant to.

'It's his heart,' she explained, putting her arms round me, then round several others, letting them kiss her cheeks while she kissed the air. In her progress I noticed her take a step towards Charlie, who was next in the line, then see him. 'Not you, dear,' she said and changed direction.

While I was arranging the set I heard Charlie saying to Molly, 'This fellow? Your husband, isn't he? What's he got against me?'

I had a fast serve and foolishly I let my feelings get into it. This gave Charlie the excuse to turn his back and make remarks about professionalism. In the third game I hit him full toss half-way up the thigh. For the rest of the afternoon, whenever he saw me watching him he started to limp heavily, glowering sideways with mock fury. He knew how angry it was making me because he knew it hadn't been an accident.

Annoyingly, Charlie could play well. Without moving much he made good shots and placed them cleverly. Molly played as she always did, with absent-minded talent. I loved her best when she pretended she'd intended some killing shot which hurried down the sideline, five yards from the nearest opponent. Rene was hopeless. She played – the phrase came to me instinctively – like someone whose nerve had gone. In command of her regiment I'd have returned her to base before she deserted in the face of the enemy.

Near the close of the set I saw, with a relief which surprised me, Janie and Jim Brightworth coming up the drive. I wanted to go and meet them. If I had had suspicions of Jim they were then totally dissolved.

I was surprised that Janie had come, knowing what she thought of Englishmen playing games. 'Look at them wasting themselves,' I'd heard her say, too upset to enjoy her anger. Certainly she had no intention of playing and wore a summer dress almost too narrow at the knees for her to walk, let alone run. It was a bright blue tube, with nothing above her breasts, showing all her olive brown neck, shoulders and arms. Below it she wore only expensive soft leather sandals. It was an outfit which on anyone else would have seemed like fancy dress. Strangely, a point or two later when we'd all seen her, the game did come to a spontaneous pause and we moved to meet them.

'It's awful,' Janie said. I think she was genuinely embarrassed.

'Cute, isn't she,' Jim shouted, taking a playful swing at her buttocks with his racket.

'You *like* it?' Janie said, as if willing for a second to be persuaded. 'Oh, you can't.' And she went to sit by herself in a deckchair. We all watched but didn't follow because Jim stood with arms and racket raised to keep us back. 'Hands off there.'

Only then did I see Hubert Brightworth sloping into our drive. He must have been following them thirty yards behind. I was astonished but also flattered.

I guessed that after he'd decided to come he'd seen his mother's dress and refused, till he'd thought of this compromise. Whenever I noticed him that afternoon he seemed to be looking carefully away from it.

From then on things got worse. They seemed to be slipping out of my control, or more exactly, out of my view. If two people visited us I knew what was happening. Even when I was talking to one of them and Molly to the other I had a sense of what was going on. If there were more I lost touch. I was aware that jokes were being told which I didn't understand or people laughing when I hadn't even heard anything said. I got angry. I wanted to drive them away.

That was what happened that afternoon. And gradually it seemed that all this laughing and talking which I couldn't properly hear was one big joke, a joke they were all sharing, a joke about me.

It had sometimes occurred to me that I was liked by our local friends because I amused them. They thought me slow and serious and rather stupid and I hadn't tried too hard to change this impression but even found myself encouraging it by saying slowly and seriously things which referred to subjects of conversation that had been left behind. I think I had wanted them to laugh so that they would not be alarmed by mistaking me for an intellectual. This laughter was nothing like that. It was hostile and jeering.

When Mrs. Willis arrived it seemed to increase. I began to feel a great pressure inside my head. As a boy I'd often had this feeling, but not for many years. It wasn't painful – at first. It just felt as if it might burst.

I couldn't think what Mrs. Willis was dressed for, certainly not a cup of tea beside a tennis lawn. She had a grey hat with pink artificial flowers and a veil with quarter-inch black spots. Her grey dress, of thick material, came to her wrists but ended above her grey-stockinged knees. She was thickly powdered. She suggested a Victorian woman at her own divorce case, who hadn't decided whether she wanted to provoke the judge's sympathy or lust. She seemed to become the centre of this conspiracy of laughter.

Gathered round her, apparently watching but actually saying

things to each other, they were secretly convulsed. But they never let a flicker of this show. I couldn't even catch them speaking, though I tried out of the corner of my eye and several times turned suddenly when they wouldn't expect it.

Molly was there. That upset me, though because she was filling and passing tea cups she might not be part of it. I couldn't tell. The only other person it seemed to upset was Jim. He was part of it but occasionally he would point his racket at me and cry, 'Look at old Harry there.' He did it at less and less appropriate moments.

I was playing singles with Rene. I should have beaten her easily but I couldn't concentrate. Suddenly I was having an idea about Jim Brightworth. It was the way he alone went on calling to me as if to include me that roused my suspicions; which shows that you can be too clever.

I was wondering whether, under my nose, I'd been failing to see, not the triple bluff of which I'd suspected Draycott, nor the double bluff of which I'd suspected Quorum, but a simple bluff. Someone whom I'd never suspected because he was obviously brainless, but who was simply acting brainless and acting very well.

Without insistence I tried out the idea. It began to take hold. I thought of what I might have to do to Jim Brightworth. I served a double fault. Then I knew I could do it. If I was right I would want to do it.

The set ended, I took my tea and walked about. I wanted to be alone. But I was glad we'd given this tennis party. I was alarmed to think how ignorant I might have stayed.

Now I seemed to be watching them again, as well as them me. Perhaps I had been imagining things.

'Cake, dear?' Molly called.

'In a minute.' I walked to the edge of the lawn and looked out over the low lands to those white and black clouds towering behind the far hills. The thunder still grumbled though it had come no nearer.

Peggy brought me a slice on a plate.

But instead of joining them I carried it with me across the foot of the court to the drive, as if to fetch something from the house.

I was five paces on to the gravel when I saw Percy Goyle. He was standing at my drive gate, looking in.

Later I wondered why Percy had been in the New Lane at that time. Pekes had to be exercised, of course, and I'd often seen him doing that. But why had he been staring up my drive? It wasn't as detached as I'd have expected. At the time I assumed that something incidental to my tennis party must have caught his attention, the swallows flying close above the lawn, or a passing hover-fly.

'Hallo,' I called. 'Come and have some tea.'

When his peke heard me it stopped snuffling and also stared. It gave a couple of preliminary yaps, flexing its knees in time. I think I had the idea that I would use Percy Goyle to break up the others. I could lead him to them, talking casually to him.

It worked. As soon as I brought him across they ceased to be united and began to talk in pairs. I was able, quite naturally, to talk now to one, now to another of them. At the same time I could hear other conversations going on around me, for instance Jim and Percy Goyle.

'You should have a bash,' Jim said.

'Oh no.'

'You don't know what it's like till you've tried.'

'No no.'

'Here, I'll teach you.'

'No, really, no.'

'Never too late. You've certainly got the reach.' But he saw he was losing.

'Anyway I have tried,' Percy said.

'You've played,' Jim said. 'Well, there you are!'

'I think so,' Percy said. He seemed less sure, now that he had heard the improbable idea said aloud. 'A long time ago.'

'Well, what are we waiting for?' Jim said.

They went on and on. It was as if Jim had found a better contact with Percy than he had ever found before and had to keep touching it in case he lost it. It was as if he were intent on showing himself as stupidly insensitive as possible. Had he always overacted in this way?

Presently I had an idea. I see how rash this was and can only suppose that at the time I was puffed up with conceit at my discovery.

'Do you make cheese?' I said, in the general direction of Mrs. Willis though not so that she could be certain I meant it for her. At once the other conversations around me were stopping with astonishment.

'What, me?' Mrs. Willis said. She glanced left and right as if hoping for someone else to answer. That was something I foolishly thought unimportant but at the time I was only interested in the way Wilfred was nervously rubbing his ear with a bandaged hand and Charlie had forgotten to finish a joke about de Gaulle and Jim had actually let his mouth fall open as he listened.

'Out of sour milk,' I went on, enjoying myself, I admit.

'I certainly do not,' Mrs. Willis said, recovering now. 'Disgusting.'

'It's the right weather,' I said casually, as if the subject had become a bore.

By this time the others were also recovering.

'Oh but it's lovely,' Rene said.

'Well to be honest . . .' Wilfred began.

'Fermented with camel's urine,' Charlie said.

They were too late. As if to support me, there was a long distant roll of thunder and for a moment of silence we all listened to it. Or rather they listened and I watched them. At once I was applying to Jim the old theory about size of nose varying with size of penis. I'd always thought it biological nonsense but, staring at Jim's huge nose, I realized that about Jim I instinctively believed it. No doubt my momentary preoccupation took my attention from the conversation and by the time I listened again it was general and unimportant. It didn't matter. I'd learned more than I'd hoped.

After tea I watched. Hubert was playing. He played in black shoes with shirt sleeves buttoned. Without his glasses he was like a nocturnal animal put out in the daylight. It wasn't till six when the afternoon was getting cooler and the sun going down that I next played.

As soon as I got on to the court my suspicions returned. The joke had begun again. But this time they weren't together in a united group. They were laughing in pairs round the shadowy edges of the court. This time there was Percy as well.

It was essential that I should call on the Brightworths. Time was short. Ideally I'd have liked them to be away, as the Draycotts had been. That sort of luck didn't happen twice.

The fine weather had come again. It had never really gone. Just that afternoon of distant thunder. Perhaps the sun took a few minutes longer to grow warm in the morning. And more often there was morning mist in the low lands over my orchards, hinting at the autumn which was coming. The dews were heavy, making the lawn as wet as a shower. By ten o'clock they were forgotten and by midday the temperature was in the eighties. The flowers drooped in their beds; I'd not seen that before. I found several long cracks where the lawn had split. I liked it. I've always liked the heat. It made me feel more alive.

Molly didn't like it. It made her tired and she looked pale. She was too fair to sit in the sun, though she liked wearing big hats. Our children had other, more interesting things to like or dislike – more adult things.

I was upstairs making a few final plans till I could go when I heard voices below. There was Molly's voice, light and puzzled; she seemed to be listening more than talking. And there was a heavy voice. I got Peggy's window open without a sound and eased my shaving mirror out behind the curtain. I couldn't see Molly because she was in the doorway. Facing it stood the two policemen with their bicycles.

I listened but I could make no sense of it. I heard phrases like, 'There it is then,' and 'It's certainly a problem.' Often I heard only silence, as if they were all thinking. I heard one of them say, 'Your husband has a gun?' I went downstairs.

A few paces into the hall I came in sight of the front door. Already, in the seconds I had been coming, the conversation had ended and they had begun to mount their bicycles. I came past Molly into the doorway but now they were in wobbly flight. 'Good morning,' I called.

'Morning, sir,' they said, glancing round, but only for a second before concentrating again on the stones and ruts. I had the feeling that they wanted to come back but this problem was intervening and then the moment had passed. Using their brakes and working their handlebars they let themselves be carried out of sight round the north side of the house towards the back drive.

'What did they want?' I said.

She paused for a second. I knew those pauses. 'The rabbits,' she said.

It was far too improbable. I believed her at once.

'Someone's complained.'

'But that's fantastic,' I said. 'There isn't a hole on the place.'

She didn't argue.

'Who's complained?' I said. 'We haven't a single neighbouring farmer.'

'You have to control them,' she said.

'What was the first thing they said?' I asked.

'Just that,' she said. She seemed to be growing increasingly nervous. I had an idea that it would be easy to drive her away from the truth, less because she didn't want to tell it than because she would be too upset to be able to concentrate on it.

'Didn't I hear something about a gun?' I said gently.

'That's right,' she said. It seemed to relieve her. I thought she wanted to smile but she was still worried. 'That was how they began.'

I was appalled by this new and, as far as I could see, totally unnecessary lie. I didn't know where to start.

'You're sure?' I said. I hurried on, afraid how my doubt might affect her. 'I mean it seemed to me . . .'

'Oh, they went back to it,' she said with increasing confidence. 'I think they wanted to help. They wanted to make sure you had one. For shooting them,' she added, growing doubtful again.

I can't explain why I found this final and unnecessary information particularly shocking.

As I went down our drive I tried to make sense of it. To my right I could hear Dan and Peggy beyond the court on the hillside, shouting among the trees. Close on my left there was a sharp snap which made my hand close in my empty pocket and I hesitated about going back at least for a knife, but it was only a broom pod snapping in the sun. I could make nothing of it.

I forced myself to think of the job ahead. I went over some of the ideas I'd had in the almost sleepless night which had followed yesterday's tennis. First was the fact that genuine stupid hearties don't succeed in commerce. They make good salesmen but they don't buy the business as Jim had done.

Second, I couldn't any longer see Jim's behaviour as the behaviour of a real person. The two had come apart in a way I couldn't control so that even if someone had said to me, 'That's what he's like, those are real words coming out of him,' I wouldn't have been able to fit him to them any more.

But it wasn't till I'd crossed the New Lane and was in his drive that I saw the really obvious clue which had been right in front of me all summer. I saw it when I realized that I wouldn't find Jim at the house. He was taking his holiday at home, he'd told me, to finish his swimming pool. His swimming pool . . .

The hours he spent down there, the digging and concreting – my mind was confused by the possibilities. The way he'd discouraged visits till it was done, the time it had taken. It had been happening literally under my eyes, for I could see the grey shapes and piles of sand through the treetops from my attic window. And except that once when he'd escorted me, I'd made no attempt to investigate it.

I stopped dead. I was shivering again. And the only thought in my mind, it cannot be. Surely I am playing some dangerous game with myself.

But how could I know? I had again an overpowering urge to hunt in my real memory for something which would prove to me that my whole life was not – nonsense. The word terrified me. I half understood that the terror I now felt about not believing was like the terror I had once felt about believing, half understood because I would not let myself recognize the parallel. I began as I had not for years to try to remember what had really happened. In my search I seemed to reach a peak of assurance when I held a memory in its original genuineness, a memory of those first answering signals I had had when I bought and learned to use my transmitter. They were something I knew had really happened. Immediately I suffered the greatest doubt. Real doubt? Or doubt I had trained myself to feel? How could I tell?

At that moment, with a force that I had not felt before, I knew that I really didn't know. I understood for the first time that the muddle in my memory was such that I could never sort it out. I was close to tears. I wanted to cry out to someone for help. There wasn't anyone.

Just the Brightworths' house ahead down their drive. A step at a time, my knees shaking, I began to move on towards it. To the right of its white concrete façade, in its own white concrete box, I saw the chrome bumpers and polished boot of Jim's Jaguar. A second later Jim was at the door. That was my first surprise.

I hadn't realized how my feelings for him had changed. When I saw him there I was filled with hate. Of course this was partly anger at the way he had deceived me for so many years. But it was also anger with him as a person, a mock person, someone who stood for all I hated most. I hated him for the way he reduced conversation to animal noises – or animal buffetings. I hated his ostrich-head digging and burrowing. I hated him as much for what he pretended so successfully to be as for what he really was – the full implications of that I was still guessing.

'Hallo, there,' he shouted.

'So you're in,' I said foolishly.

'That's it,' he shouted. 'Didn't expect that, did you?' Though he watched me as he said this I had the idea that he was thinking about something else.

'It's normal,' I began.

'Normal!' Jim said. 'Never met him. Ha ha, caught you there.'

'I mean . . .' I began.

'Trying to get out of it, aren't you,' he said, taking my hand. Instead of letting go when he'd shaken it he pulled me towards him, so that I stumbled up the steps right past him into the house. It gave me a moment of panic.

'That's the way,' I heard him shout behind me. 'Come right in. Don't wait to be asked.' I realized that it was his new joke. Janie was in the hall.

'Well, hallo,' she cried, coming towards me with spontaneous warmth.

'Wo ho, there,' Jim shouted behind me. 'Give a chap a chance. Wait till he's out of his own front door.'

I didn't laugh or turn. If I'd turned I might have hit him.

'Come right in,' Janie said, taking me by the hand to the sitting-room. 'Bring us some drinks, dearest.'

'Look at them,' Jim said. 'Caught red-handed and this is what they do.'

'Go away, you noisy brute,' Janie said. She led me to the sofa and we sat together. 'Tell me all about it,' she said.

The question appalled me. I had an increasing sense of not understanding what was happening. For perhaps a minute I couldn't speak.

I forced myself to answer. 'Well,' I began. It was a dry croak. I cleared my throat and pretended to choke. For several minutes I spluttered and she patted my back. As I sat with my hand to my mouth, recovering, I saw, through the mauve glass of an irregular hexagonal window, Hubert on the lawn. The glass distorted him so that by moving my head a fraction of an inch I could make his grey trousers expand and contract several feet, but for some reason I could never reach his shoes. He was kicking at something on the lawn but this too was out of sight.

Jim brought a tray with glasses and a jug full of Pimms and submerged green leaves with a silver Pimms strainer.

'Well, I don't know!' he shouted. 'Comes to the door. More or less passes out from shock when I open it. Then goes right ahead.'

'Bring some ice, there's a dear,' Janie said, but she took her arm off the sofa above my back.

I pulled myself together. I was getting nowhere. 'I came to ask if you'd give me a golf lesson,' I said.

I watched him narrowly. He was putting ice into the glasses with a silver spoon. 'I've heard it called some funny things,' he said. He stood up to give me a stare of mock astonishment. 'Well!' he said as if increasingly amazed. He gave several high and I thought slightly hysterical laughs.

'Why did I marry this vulgar man?' Janie said.

I laughed a bit. 'If it's a trouble . . .'

'Trouble!' Jim said. 'No trouble, except I don't play.' He drank with his elbow lifted high and stared.

I listened hard. Was I imagining it or had Janie on the sofa beside me also started to listen hard.

'Last time I lifted a club was way back, let me see, way back . . .'

'Oh what a liar he is,' Janie said.

'Liar!' Jim said. 'Who said that?'

Unfortunately my attention was distracted by a movement in that mauve hexagonal window. It was Hubert who had come much closer on the lawn so that I could only see him from the chest up, though it occurred to me that the glass might be magnifying him and he was really farther away. Now he was looking directly towards me through his big spectacles, but I had the impression that he couldn't see me, as if the glass was one way. By moving my head the smallest amount I could reduce his chest to a couple of inches or expand it three feet.

'You don't call that golf!' Jim was saying, and I realized with fury that I'd missed the vital seconds. 'That was to prove I could wake up before midday. That was because Charlie said I'd never seen any dew. Now Charlie, he's a real golfer. Ask Charlie.'

I'd barely time to guess at the implications of this when a bell rang. I was closer to the room door than Janie sitting beside me, or Jim bending over her glass, pouring Pimms, holding back leaves with the silver strainer. 'I'll go,' I said.

I was out of the room in a second, so that I had no chance to judge their alarm. I had to hurry, in case their Spanish maid came from the kitchen. I turned the latch soundlessly and opened the front door suddenly. It was Wilfred Draycott.

His hands were still heavily bandaged, though his left one was no longer in a sling. He still had the plaster on his nose. The consternation on his face was funny. It seemed the clearest piece of evidence I'd yet had. It was typical that Wilfred should provide it.

'You here?' he said.

I checked myself, quickly realizing that he had a good reason for showing surprise when the wrong person opened the wrong front door. Perhaps he hadn't been so foolish.

'Could be,' I said. 'You bringing the post?'

He was carrying a slim envelope of unfolded foolscap size. 'Oh, that,' he said, glancing at it, smiling casually.

What he didn't realize was that I'd noticed the instinctive movement of his bandaged hand to hide it behind him the moment he'd seen me at the door. He'd checked it, of course, but not soon enough.

'Yes, that,' I said.

He glanced at it again. When I didn't get out of the doorway, he began to stare at me as if surprised by my rude curiosity. He didn't stare me in the eyes but in the middle of my chest. 'That's something I've been doing for Jim.'

It was well judged. It would have been suspicious if he'd told me more. I let him pass. Unfortunately he blocked my view as he went into the sitting-room so that I could see no sign which may have passed between them.

'I've brought you the designs,' I heard him say. He put the envelope on the triangular table, with the ebony top and brass tube legs.

'Thanks,' Jim said. 'Have a drink. It's a party. Didn't you know?'

But I was hardly listening, too amazed by Wilfred's careless words. Either their self-confidence was colossal, or, still more alarming, it no longer mattered what I guessed. I watched closely when Jim poured me more Pimms. I watched his hand for any powder he might feed from below it into my glass.

I saw nothing, but before I drank I passed behind the settee and casually held it to the light. There was a mush of fruit at the top and bubbles rising from the sides but the bottom seemed clear. I sipped.

'Come on then, don't hold back,' Jim said. It made me jump badly. A second later I realized he was talking to Wilfred about his envelope. I shut my mouth, which had fallen open.

'I don't want to be a bore,' Wilfred began.

'Aw, come on,' Jim said. He made a move towards the envelope. The telephone rang.

I hadn't noticed it before. It was ivory, with red number sockets. It purred on an ivory shelf. 'Hallo there,' Jim called into it. Putting his hand over the mouthpiece he stage-whispered to us, 'C. Quorum, Esq.'

But I could scarcely attend for, to add to my astonishment that I should have chanced to walk in on this gathering, I was now amazed to see Wilfred Draycott reapproaching his envelope, lifting it from the table.

'Come on over,' Jim was shouting. 'Haven't they told you? It's a party.' He was opening the flap. He was peering in. He was inserting a bandaged hand.

'Aw, forget it,' Jim called. 'You've got a convert. Thought he'd come to seduce my wife. Not a bit of it. Only interested in the life of sport. The tee, the fairway, the green. We can hardly hold him. His hands keep twitching. His eyes have that faraway look.'

Whenever he paused I could imagine Charlie being dryly witty, or allowing dryly witty silences. I could imagine how Jim was missing these. But all the time my eyes were on that thin sheaf of foolscap sheets which Wilfred had extracted and was now looking at, as if wondering for the first time how they might seem to someone else.

When Janie asked he showed them to her. She held them, looking at the top sheet, but neither she nor Jim, when he held them, showed the slightest curiosity about the undersheets which they were also holding.

Looking past their arms I saw four ink sketches, each in a different way showing a bird of prey perched on a box.

'Smashing,' Jim said. 'Aren't they good?' He turned to me. 'Don't you like them? Be honest. Which do you like? Which stinks least?'

Suddenly I understood: Jim's business, The Peregrine Packaging Company Limited. They were Peregrines sitting on packages. It was some new crest or trademark.

A hint at a time, Jim told me.

'Never pay if you've got a friend.'

'In due course . . .' Wilfred began.

'He thinks he's going to catch my account,' Jim said. 'Put me under a moral obligation. What's that? Ever heard of it?' He gave me a huge wink. 'Here, drink up.' He advanced on me with the Pimms jug.

'No really, thanks.'

'What are we then? A bunch of Sabattarians?'

'I didn't want a second,' I said. 'Sorry to waste it. Unless you . . .' I began, holding it towards him.

'What, me!' Jim said. 'I wouldn't dare.'

'Wouldn't dare?'

'Didn't you know?' Janie called. 'Jim's got a suspected ulcer.'

I had to leave. I was sure I'd seen him drinking a moment before, though when I looked for his glass I couldn't see it. I had again that horrible sense that I was being laughed at. My head was swelling, swelling.

'Don't go, you there,' Janie said, holding my hand.

'I must.' I forced it free and hurried out. I was escaping but I felt no triumph. I felt like a victim of their charity.

As I left the room I heard Wilfred say modestly, 'There're a few more.' Turning my head, I caught a glimpse of lifting sheets. On the lower sheets I saw more box designs.

I must have been a bit dazed as I walked home. Perhaps it was the bright hot sunlight after their house. It wasn't till I reached the New Lane that I realized what had disturbed me about those under sheets. They'd had boxes but there'd been no birds on them. I was almost certain.

Boxes. It was the sight of my house and the memory of what had last happened there that morning which gave me the clue. What else could be kept in wooden boxes? At once I was making sense of the whole vicious plan. What better and more innocent way to distract and sabotage me than to arrange in these vital days for me to be preoccupied with some stupid police prosecution?

I had been right. There had been no rabbits in my orchard – till a few days ago.

Suddenly I was reassessing that absurd story about Wilfred and the cucumber frames, remembering that hanging cupboard, so obviously his own horrible handiwork, that moment in the dusk when he had held up what looked like a saw. Wilfred had been carpentering. Converting wooden boxes. Adding doors with wire netting, and solid fronts for nesting compartments. And I was seeing new sense in that strange early-morning golfing expedition along the edge of the course which bordered my land. It was an inspection of their releasing grounds. I was still testing these ideas when I met Molly.

She was ten yards from the gate of our drive, coming towards me.

'I couldn't find you,' she said.

'I was calling on Jim,' I said. 'I wanted him to give me some golf lessons.'

'Does he play?' she said.

'Not much,' I said.

I could tell from the way she didn't answer that she'd already forgotten her question. We started to walk together.

'The telephone rang,' she said.

'Who was it?'

'No one.'

'They weren't there?' I asked.

But again her mind had hurried away in some frightening direction where I couldn't follow.

'They do that, don't they?' she said.

'Burglars?' I said. 'To see if you're out?'

She nodded impatiently.

'So we're told,' I said. 'I don't know if I believe it.'

She didn't answer.

'Was there any sound?' I asked.

'Just a click,' she said. 'The second I lifted it. Then the dialling tone.'

That was a bad day. My head got worse.

Why had she come to find me? Or had she been on her way to the Brightworths' house, like so many other people that morning? What had she really thought when the telephone had rung, then clicked and buzzed? Or had that really happened at all?

Before lunch I hurried down my hillside. In the orchard nearest to the golf course there were many small scrapings of the sort rabbits make when pursuing a tasty root. True I hadn't looked for them lately, but I was sure I'd have noticed. I hunted in the hedges but could find no holes. I hurried back to the house.

All that afternoon I listened for the telephone.

PART FIVE

I HEARD it that evening. I was in the back drive, looking north. I ran.

I took it in the office. I lifted the receiver and at once I heard the disconnecting click. I worked the rest, giving the ready-to-receive flashes. There was a second's pause, then the steady buzz began. I could hear nothing else. As I sat at the office desk, holding the receiver to my ear, looking out through the open door at the sunlit lawn, I heard steps and Molly was coming past.

'What is it?' She stopped at the doorway, staring in. Her eyes were frightened.

Perhaps what frightened her was the look of drawn worry which I had allowed to come on my face. I relaxed it quickly. I made a sign for her to be quiet, as if I was listening. I put my hand over the mouthpiece and said, 'I'm not sure.' I took it away and went on listening. I was starting to hear things.

For a second more she stared in, then went away.

As when they'd given me the escape procedure I was hearing them through the dialling tone which never stopped. The difference was that they were fainter, as if they had gone much farther away.

They were so faint that I wondered if they'd been there all the time but I'd not been listening with enough care. At first I couldn't hear what they were saying. Then I caught it. 'Beware H.Q. Beware H.Q. Beware H.Q.'

They went on like that for perhaps a minute and then without warning stopped. I gave the receiver a shake, I can't think why. I said, 'Are you there?' Again I flashed the ready-to-receive combination. Nothing happened. I was worried and frightened.

I went into the garden. I showed myself to Molly as I went, as if with purpose, across the lawn towards the tennis court.

'What happened?'

'Nothing,' I said, going on towards the tennis net which I lowered.

Passing her more slowly on the way back I said, 'Perhaps it's out of order.'

'Do you think so?'

'Could be.'

'Then why does it ring?'

'Some fault which disconnects us as soon as it's lifted.'

She wasn't convinced, but she thought I might believe it.

I went from place to place in the garden, trying to work it out. Who or what was H.Q.? It wasn't our word for the central organization. It stood for no local place I could think of.

I tried not to let Molly see how I was moving restlessly about with nothing to do, but twice she noticed me and I think she guessed. I went into the house. Perhaps I should go to my attic, but at that time of day it would be unusual.

It was a warning, that was all I could tell. There was something desperate about the far-off way it had come to me and the way it had been cut off.

We had supper. The telephone was still worrying her, I could tell. I was irritated that she should be worried, giving me this new burden. It passed and I talked to the children.

I had to do the talking. They were oddly silent. Usually it was easy to start their interests but that night they just ate, looking at their plates. They didn't seem to have quarrelled.

Dusk settled on the house and garden. They were undressing, then in bed. I stood in the veranda, looking out at the darkening lawns and bushes. I sat in the sitting-room, leaving the french windows open, and picked up a book. Molly was reading but noticing. It grew chilly and I shut the french windows.

I had just sat down again when I saw him. It was like a relief. At the same moment that I caught my breath I wanted to sigh with the relief of it.

He was in the bed of shrubs across the lawn. Because of the bright lights inside and the dusk outside he was hard to see. He stood upright and quite still. I found that complete stillness shocking. It told me he was an expert who knew that people see movements, not things. Even now when I had seen him his stillness made me doubtful.

I knew at once that I must get out there. Sitting here, I was an animal in a cage. He could move where he wanted, do what he wanted and I would lose him. I couldn't move to any place where he couldn't see me and guess what I was doing. If I drew the curtains he'd be able to come closer with still less caution. Whatever room I went to, I'd know he might be looking in through the cracks.

Already I was losing him. He might still be there, in the shadows beyond the peonies. Or was what I was now seeing the shape of a young birch? Had he already slipped down the bank, made a quick transit out of sight, and reached the bushes behind the back door where he could examine the drain-pipes and gutters leading to the upper windows?

There were two problems: first, to give Molly a sensible reason for leaving the room when I'd just begun to read; second, to get out of the house without letting him see me and yet do nothing which Molly would hear and think odd, like climbing through the lavatory window. Yet I knew that none of our outside doors could be opened without a noise. I'd left them like that in case one day they gave me a vital second of warning.

I stretched and stood.

I went to the kitchen and stoked. I climbed swiftly to the attic and got my red night-adaptation goggles. In the kitchen again I rattled the stove door and scraped at the coke with the shovel as if I'd been there all the time. If Molly came out I'd slip the goggles into a pocket.

I went to the lavatory and pulled the chain. Not a sound from the sitting-room. You can do a lot of suspicious things under people's noses. Even if they notice, their minds busily fit reasonable explanations to them. They're on your side, most of the time, helping you cover up.

Now came the moment when I'd have to trust that she'd ceased to listen. I went through the scullery and out through the inner back door. It led to a six-foot passage with the larder on one side and steps to the coal store on the other. I went down these and crossed in pitch darkness to the hatch where the coal is delivered. Everything I touched felt black and sooty. A sooty sack brushed my face. It couldn't be helped. It might be useful.

Pushing above my shoulders I lifted the hatch and slid it sideways. From the piled coal I climbed through the opening into a small shed. I crouched and listened. It was dark here, too, but some faint light was coming through a cobweb-hung window. Using both hands I carefully lifted the door latch and stepped out.

I took off the goggles. Full adaptation takes half an hour, and I was still short of that, but the rapid stage is over in two minutes. As soon as I had them off I could see well. I shut my eyes – not to help the adaptation but to listen.

Below on the main road I heard three cars pass. On the common far away on the other side of the house an owl called. That was all.

I had to get away from the house. I might blunder into him, of course, but I must risk that. Stepping quietly, though in a casual way, I went down the back path, joined the back drive and followed it to the New Lane. I didn't see a thing.

I stood close to the drive gate in the darkness below a Scots pine, looking down the New Lane as if at the after glow of the sunset which was still orange above the hills. It was quiet and beautiful. The stars were coming out.

Looking back I saw the half moon above the dark shape of the house. Soon it would give me more light than the fading day. I dropped into the bushes. I'd practised that. One moment I'd be there, the next gone, swallowed up, moving without a sound, already thirty feet away.

I circled the house. I did it slowly and thoroughly.

I kept among the shrubs and bushes all the way and this made it a long job. Only for three seconds was I in the open, going like a shadow across the front drive. To avoid the lawns I had to circle the tennis court. All the time as I went I could hear that owl, calling far below on the common.

There were three lights in the house and they never changed. One was Molly's, reading in the sitting-room. Directly above was Dan's. He must be reading in bed. And one was the light I'd left burning in the hall at the foot of the stairs. Molly's and Dan's I could see only from the lawn side. The hall light I could see from several directions, sometimes the lit shade itself, sometimes a yellow glow through opaque glass, sometimes a faint greyness where it was shining through a doorway on to the wall of another room.

I could find no one in the garden. I didn't think anyone was there. Of course they might have been moving ahead of me, or have crouched still as I passed. I didn't think so. The garden didn't feel as if there was anyone in it. It felt as if they'd gone.

I must have grown tired towards the end of that long circuit. My back and legs ached. I wanted to stretch them but didn't dare. I began to stumble and make noises.

It was dark now, except in the moonlight. Before I could rejoin the back drive there was a thick slope where this didn't reach. There were brambles here and I wasn't seeing them, and they were catching in my clothes and legs. Twice I ducked my head into branches I hadn't seen and a twig went into my eye.

I began to feel pursued. If there was anyone near, they could hardly fail to hear me, moving through the bushes like a blind animal. I wanted to keep still, then go silently so that they would lose me. I didn't dare. I was more and more worried about the time I had taken. At last I was clear and stood at the foot of the back drive below the Scots pine, where I had stood almost an hour before.

I thought there was someone in the New Lane. I thought I heard a snuffling noise. Every time I seemed to catch it for certain it stopped. I thought a shadow moved. At that moment a car came by and I ducked out of its headlights. If anyone was there they must have ducked, too, for the yellow cone of light which came up the lane between the black trees was empty.

I went quietly up the back drive and tried the back door. It was locked. I'd forgotten that I'd done that.

Or had Molly locked it? Had she made a circuit of the house doors, assuming I was in bed? Suddenly it was an awkward problem. If I knocked I would have to explain what I'd been doing out here for so long. But if I came in through the coal hatch I might astonish her still more if by now she had realized that I was out and was waiting for my knock.

I came in through the coal hatch, less because I knew the answer than because I didn't yet want to face her.

It made me uneasy to be inside again. I blinked in the hall light. The sitting-room door was shut and there was a bright line below it. There was no light upstairs. I climbed quietly to our bedroom. No one was there.

I thought of going to the cellar to get my .38 with the silencer from the safe. I could put it between the lower and upper mattresses on my side of the bed. I'd feel safer – suddenly there was someone in the garden again.

Perhaps I'd seen a movement outside the bedroom window – I hadn't turned on the light. Crouching against the wall I peered over the sill. The window was open on the warm summer night. Presently I could see them. I was almost sure.

If only I'd had the gun. It wouldn't have been easy to aim in the dark, with the front sight invisible. I laid my hand on the sill, aiming carefully along my finger. I could have done it.

There'd have been no disturbing noise. Perhaps I should still fetch it. But it seemed too soon, and too uncertain. I'd been told to take care, but not to fire wildly about my garden at unknown people.

I might fire a warning shot, to show that I wasn't a blind fool. But a silent gun wouldn't do that. Presently I saw that it would be a mistake anyway. Not to be a fool was one thing. To show you weren't was another – and perhaps a foolish thing.

For five minutes I crouched there. I could still see his shape. He kept quite still. Then I was less sure. I went quietly up to my attic, and came down loudly. I came down to the sitting-room.

She was reading and didn't look up. I locked the french windows and collected the pages of newspaper to carry out.

'Good book?'

'Ah ha.' She went on reading, then looked at me, but she was still with the book. She smiled and stretched, coming out of it.

'Wherever have you been?'

I went on bundling the newspapers. I let one catch my attention. 'What's that?' I said.

'You're black.'

'Am I?' I'd been mad to forget it. Then it was suddenly easy. 'I was fetching some coke.'

'You certainly were.' She came close, her eyes laughing. She didn't try to brush it, as if there was too much.

'And you've got heather in your hair.'

'In my hair . . .'

'Yes,' she said. 'There's heather in your hair.' Her eyes weren't laughing.

I shrugged my shoulders. 'God knows.' I carried the newspaper to the kitchen cupboard, as if irritated by the way she'd been examining me.

Late that night I called them. The procedure was clear and simple. Any time of day or night in the past years I could have done it. Of course I hadn't – except for the two-monthly checks, and they were routine. There'd been no need.

Now that my danger was increasing I had to pass on what I knew. I couldn't let it go with me. Perhaps they knew already, but I felt this less likely as the web of intrigue I was uncovering grew more complex.

By explaining things I might get them clear in my own mind.

I drew my attic curtains, leaving no cracks. I knelt on the floor and raised the three floorboards. I twisted the knobs and listened. I kept the volume down; the children's bedrooms were below and though they were asleep I didn't know what they might wake and hear and mention next morning. I would, of course, use a throat microphone, so that I could completely muffle my voice in a pad of cottonwool and still transmit my words. I strapped it on.

I was getting the receiving signal. It seemed faint but that was because I had the volume low.

I held the pad to my mouth and spoke. 'H.1. reporting. Category urgent. No medium urgent.' I took the pad from my mouth and carefully cleared my throat. I must be exact and short. Above all I must show none of the panic I was starting to feel. I tried to gather my thoughts, but they seemed to be hurrying here and there, unable to settle on a point to start. All the time I could hear the faint receiving signal.

I spoke into the pad. 'Unable identify watcher. Suspect many at work. Require instructions, view short time remaining.' I stopped. It wasn't what I'd meant to say. I'd meant to tell them about Draycott and Quorum and Brightworth and how I was unable to decide which or how many of them were involved.

Suddenly I was angry that they should tell me so little, angry and frightened in case they were to tell me no more. How could I operate usefully without information? I spoke into the pad. 'Have gathered full details of local build-up. Await firm instructions action required.'

I could hardly be more blunt. Now they could ask me if they wanted. I wasn't going to make myself a fool by telling them things they already knew. I crouched and listened.

The receiving signal went on tweeting faintly down there between the floor joists. It worried me. I'd expected that if ever I had anything to pass there'd be a real reply.

It had been a foolish idea. They'd received my message. That was all there was to say. They weren't there to make small talk, nor was I here to expect it. I closed the floorboards, switched off the light, let myself out of the attic and locked it. I went down through the dark house.

It was all dark except for squares of moonlight which were coming through the windows. Some fell on the stair walls. Through the open door of Peggy's room I could see some on her bed. I heard the owl.

It was louder than I'd ever heard it. I stood at the open landing window, looking out across the moonlit lawn to the pine from where I was sure it had come. I almost expected to see it but of course I couldn't.

It didn't say 'toowhit toowhoo'. I'd never heard one say that. It made a drawn-out hoot which was all one noise but a bit tremulous. Now that I was staring up towards it, it didn't hoot any more, as if it could see me.

It was like an all-clear. It wouldn't have come there if there was anyone still in the garden.

PART SIX

I HAD a bad dream that night. It wasn't the rabbits I minded, but they were all going bad. They were everywhere, of course, and I was trying to drive them off but as soon as I saw a healthy fluffy bunny rabbit and ran at it to try to drive it away it began to decay. It collapsed into a smelly decaying sticky rabbit so that I knew if I touched it it would come to pieces. And what would be left would stick to the ground. I brushed at these putrid messes but the broom only spread them; it began to stick in them. I tried to hold my breath for the foul smell which was rising. The broom was completely stuck and I strained and my heart pounded. I woke.

I lay still with my eyes closed but as soon as I drifted towards sleep I began to hold my breath and brush and strain.

Hubert came in the morning.

I was sitting in the office. Half turning in my chair I saw him coming up our drive.

It's hard to describe how Hubert walked because he walked in several ways. He kept his eyes on the ground but sometimes he took long strides and sometimes short. Sometimes he swung one arm hard but not the other. Every now and again he would give his shoulders a violent shrug. Occasionally I found myself expecting him to give a skip but he always caught himself in time. You could tell his mind wasn't on his walking, and when something stopped him he would look round as if with surprise at where he'd got to.

'Hallo, Hubert,' I called. Instinctively I wanted to help him come safely to port. Or just remind him where he was coming in case he forgot and began to go away again.

He stopped completely. Perhaps he couldn't see me, inside the office. Or perhaps even through his thick glasses I was beyond his range. Presently he changed direction and came across the lawn.

We went into the sitting-room.

'Have a drink,' I said. 'Isn't this weather marvellous.'

Hubert grunted. No one could make me feel so strongly the

futility of the things I said, the insult to speech and thought they were. It never occurred to me to patronize the young. I genuinely believed they knew better. Their brains worked better and they had more intellectual courage. They could afford it. They noticed and felt more. They were more alive, proper people. I didn't believe in maturity, except as an invention of the old to cover inferiority. Hubert made me feel about seventy and immaturing fast.

Hubert never said anything to me that wasn't in a veiled or open way offensive. And yet he would come to see me once or twice most holidays. I genuinely thought this a compliment. I didn't remember him ever telling me why he'd come. Knowing Janie and Jim I could guess but I took care never to ask.

That morning, as he stood there, grunting at his beer, insulting the things I said, I felt that he would have liked to explain why he'd come. Twice I caught him looking at me instead of the carpet. Oddly, I wanted to confide in him too, not a real confidence, but something to show him what I might have said had circumstances been different.

He stood in the french windows, shoulders hunched, thin and black against the bright garden outside. He said, 'There's going to be a party.' He couldn't bring himself to be more exact. He would have had to mention his parents.

'Fine,' I said. 'Are we invited?'

'That's it,' he said, as if astonished that I hadn't heard.

'When is it?'

But he was far away, probably didn't hear.

He said, 'It's finished.' I wish I could convey the horror he got into those words. He watched me. It was so terrible that he gave a single high guffaw.

'The swimming pool?'

He went on watching me. I think he was still surprised at the noise he'd made. I wondered if I'd ever before heard Hubert laugh. He took a dirty envelope from his pocket, handed it to me and hurried away.

It was the invitation. It was for eight on Wednesday.

I spent most of the morning on that card and its envelope. I heated them, steamed them, ironed them and rubbed them. I examined them through a microscope and soaked them in all the usual and a few unusual chemicals. Nothing showed. I still couldn't believe that Hubert had come just to deliver that party invitation. It wasn't like him to show even this much appalled co-operation with his parents' parties.

On the afternoon of the Brightworths' party I pruned Percy Goyle's blackcurrant bushes. Molly told me he wanted an expert to do it. I thought it was one of the few uncomplicated things that had happened lately. I was glad to be doing it.

I started from the farm office, where I'd gone to cross off yesterday on my calendar. I hadn't done it in the morning and as soon as I'd got there I'd seen why. When yesterday had gone there were only two clear days before the day which I'd marked with a heavy ink blot. I'd sat at my desk staring at those two blank days. One of them was today.

Not till I was beyond Percy's drive gate did I realize the madness of that calendar. I ran back. Controlling my panting I hurried across the lawn, hid it inside my shirt and stood at the office door. No one was in sight. I slipped down the back path and crossed the back drive to my pine copse. I put a match to it.

It wasn't the ink blot that had frightened me. I'd been careful enough to use that and not some obvious circle or star. It was the way I'd idiotically drawn oblique strokes through the rest of the days on that sheet and the way I'd absent-mindedly turned the pages and put a single oblique stroke across the rest of the months that year. They were about as absent-minded as the visitor a suicide invites for ten minutes after he'll have taken the pills.

I stood in the back drive, watching the pale line of smoke rising through the fir tops. It went straight up. There wasn't a breath of wind. Presently I couldn't see it any more.

It was one of those afternoons when the sun develops a haze. Though it was hazy up there it was no cooler. The opposite. As I worked with the cutters in Percy's kitchen garden the sun burnt my neck, as if the mist had the properties of a lens and was making it fiercer. The bushes were neglected and needed several main stems taken from each one, which would have been easier cut with a saw. My face ran with sweat and sometimes I could taste the salty drops and sometimes I could see them falling into the grass. I thought I must stop and stand in the shade, but I went on working.

It was the size of Percy's kitchen garden which reminded me that Percy had a gardener. Why couldn't his gardener have pruned his blackcurrants? Who had done them in other years?

I was worried after that. I wondered why I'd had no answer when I'd rung Percy's bell. I tried to calm myself: Percy had only this year realized that I was the ideal man to prune his blackcurrants. He'd never trusted his gardener's pruning. At that moment I became aware of Percy himself, standing beyond a beech hedge, watching.

I could only see him from the chest up. He gave the impression of watching not me but my work. 'Hallo,' I called.

'Hallo,' he said. He paused before he said it, as if startled that I'd noticed him.

'They're a bit neglected,' I called, to make the occasion ordinary. 'Hope you don't mind me giving them a thorough slashing.'

I saw him give such a start that I wasn't able to connect it with what I'd said. I glanced left and right for some other shocking thing which might have appeared. By the time I looked at him again he was almost out of sight, only the back of his thin grey head visible beyond the beech hedge as he hurried away. From the way it went up and down I thought he might be trotting.

I can't explain why but it made me panic. I'd felt safe while he was there. I finished the bushes in a perfunctory way and hurried down his drive to the New Lane. I was as relieved as if I'd escaped from a trap. The strange thing was, I didn't associate this trap with Percy. I felt that he had been as anxious as I was.

I felt that I had hurt him by the callous way I'd spoken about his bushes. It was as if he'd only expected a little delicate trimming and would never have asked me if he'd known I'd be so violent. Rather than what I'd done, he'd have let them grow big and useless.

Molly was on the lawn, holding the empty watering-can, looking at what she'd watered.

'That was quick.'

'Not particularly.'

I got my four-ten and went through the back door, down the hillside path. It was the wrong time of day, but there was a chance. As soon as I reached the far orchard I saw a small brown hummock. It was the shape of a rabbit nibbling, though it didn't move. The more I watched it the less clearly could I see it in that hot hazy afternoon. I raised my gun, lowered it, raised it and fired.

It must have been a long time since I'd shot because I'd forgotten how this small gun kicked. I lost sight of the hummock. I ran forward, stopped to look for it, became unsure how far away it had been. I ran back but was unsure how far I'd run forward. From wherever I looked I could see nothing like the hummock I'd fired at but neither was there any sign of a dead or struggling rabbit. I was disturbed by the memory of a spurt of dust only about ten yards in front of me. Surely that could not have been my pellets.

Now that I had made this loud noise there was less need for caution and I fired several more times at suspicious humps or shapes in the hedges. I was surprised to find that my pocket of cartridges was empty. I came up the hill path, sweating and shaking.

They were having tea in the veranda.

'Any luck?' Molly said.

I shook my head.

'We heard you shooting,' Peggy said.

'Was all that you?' Dan said.

I couldn't bear it. I went away from them back across the lawn. They must have thought it odd.

I stood beyond some trees near the tennis court, facing away from them. I should have been able to think of something to do there. The gun I still held seemed to get in the way. I glanced back through leaves. I was appalled to realize that I wasn't even out of sight.

Their tea seemed to go on and on.

I came back across the lawn towards the empty veranda. As if she had been waiting, Peggy came and stood in front of me.

'When can we go bathing?'

'What's that?'

'You promised you'd take us bathing.'

'I don't remember.'

'You did. But you won't.'

'If I promised, then I will,' I said, my anger growing.

'You won't. When will you?'

'Next week.' I was frightened as soon as I'd said it. It was a bad omen, like saying you'll win a game before you start.

'That's what you always say.'

I tried not to listen.

'But you won't.'

I tried to go past her, but now I'd seen Molly inside the french windows, watching us. Perhaps she'd been there all the time but because it was dark I hadn't seen her.

'I knew you wouldn't.'

'Shut up.' I shouted. 'I will. Didn't you hear me?'

She turned and went quickly away. I heard her say in a low voice, 'You won't.' Inside the sitting-room she stood with her face against the belly of Molly's skirt. She was crying, I knew, and Molly was probably saying things to comfort her, but for some reason I couldn't hear them in there. I saw Molly look up once towards me but she seemed more anxious than angry. I guessed she might be saying that I was worried and mustn't be bothered.

How did she know I was worried? I didn't want to hear that. It would make me want to shout at Molly too.

The people at the Brightworths' party were the same people who had come to their barbecue just eighteen days before. I knew they would be. That was why I hadn't wanted to come.

How could I speak to them about the weather and the drought and their cars when I suspected them as I did? When I was more and more aware, buried under their laughter, of how they hated me.

At six I told Molly I had a headache. It was true. It was coming in waves behind my eyes. But I needn't have told her. I registered it in case I needed it later.

Percy Goyle was there with his peke. Had he forgotten the fight it caused last time? Or didn't he think that mattered, realizing that for the dogs it had made their party? I was surprised at how relieved I felt to see him.

He stood by the fireplace (finished in smooth grey concrete in which rounded beach boulders had been set), grey and thin, watching us as we came in. I wanted to tell him that I understood how he felt about his currant bushes.

But when I stood near him I didn't try to say it. Suddenly, as if he had taught me something, I realized that this was the best, perhaps the only, way to say it. I was conscious of his calmness and sanity. I felt that if things had been different he might have given me back my trust in other people.

The Draycotts came next, without their dog. I waited to hear what had happened, uneasy not to be able to see at once evidence of some accident. Wilfred's hands were in smaller bandages.

The Quorums followed. Charlie paused dramatically at the door when he saw me. Something was coming, but I'd forgotten what. 'Careful of that man,' he said in a stage-aside to Queenie.

'What's that, dear?' Queenie said, as she came past him to give me a big hug and kiss. Beyond her I could see Charlie giving convulsive jerks of mock alarm.

'Whatever is it, dear?' she said, taking him by the arm, smiling up at him, leading him on.

'Haven't you been told?' Charlie said, not looking back, apparently careless whether or not I heard. 'The lion of the links. Hammer-drive Harry.' They went down the room, Queenie hanging on, smiling round at everyone with delight. I remembered my clever request to be taught golf. It was another mistake which was to be used against me.

Several others followed, including, rather late, Mrs. Willis. She had a hat with upright ostrich feathers, like a hussar's plume. Perhaps it was some new fashion, or perhaps it came from some thirty-year-old moth-box, or both. Like a helmet, it had straight sides which covered her ears and all her blue-rinsed hair but a coy fringe in front.

'Birdie Bale,' I heard Charlie say, and caught him giving me a quick glance then looking away with ostentatious embarrassment.

'All here, then?' Jim shouted. 'Come on, you slackers.'

'Oh, be quiet,' Janie said. 'Let's not go and see this rotten old pool.' But I guessed she was as excited about it as Jim. She no longer called it *Jim's* rotten old pool. Though she began to encourage people to dance, I thought she wanted them to insist on going.

In a ragged procession we went down the garden, through trees to the swimming pool. Dusk was coming, earlier than I'd expected, reminding me again that the month was ending. It was then that I noticed one person in the party I'd not seen before.

She was a frail, fair girl and she walked with Janie. At the same moment that I looked back and noticed her I saw Hubert shambling by himself ten yards behind everyone else, but I didn't connect them.

As soon as she saw me turn Janie called, 'Come and meet our friend Jeffy.'

I went back and met Jeffy. I must have, though it's a moment I can't clearly remember, perhaps because I was too disturbed and confused. I must have said hallo and perhaps shaken hands. I must have felt or at least seen how astonishingly frail her hand was, like a small bird's.

My feelings for Jeffy seemed to rush on me, knocking aside half a dozen usually effective barriers, leaving me facing them as amazed that it had happened as by the feelings themselves. That's the only way I can explain how I behaved that night.

As soon as we reached the pool I took her away down one side and we sat together on a stone seat.

The others stood at the far edge, looking down into the black square of water. It was much bigger than most private swimming pools, especially ones which are home dug. Everyone seemed to realize this and their chorus of exclamatory cooings sounded genuine and lasted a full minute.

Jim stood a little way from them. He wasn't making self-deprecatory noises, as I'd have expected, but listening. I wondered whether he was already feeling the shock of disappointment, now that it was finished. I asked Jeffy.

'Why, of course,' she said.

But I could only see for certain that he went on standing there and didn't hurry to fetch champagne, as Janie kept shouting at him.

Presently he said, 'Shut up. It's filled with champagne. Didn't I tell you?'

Beyond where they were standing he'd built a long wooden shelter and at its centre the barbecue was a red glow in an iron bowl on an iron tripod. The antelope skull with red bulbs for eyes hung in this open-sided shelter. They began to move towards it, holding out their hands to the fire, leaving the pool and the grass empty. And now, instead of the last pale light of day we were in moonlight. The moon was shining right into this dell-like cutting among the trees.

Clustered in that open shelter across the pool, they seemed to have gone far away from us. The popping of corks and the sizzling of steaks came out of a hum of talk which was faint and hard to hear.

We didn't join them. We didn't feel cold.

We talked in that astonishing way when understanding runs ahead of words, so that I was again imagining a moment when silence would not merely be all that was needed but something positive, which any words must reduce and contaminate. It was at once easy and terribly exacting. Sometimes I would lose track and wonder what it was all about.

Even when we crossed and mixed with them we stayed apart. We stayed together. It was less that I didn't care that everyone else should see how we were behaving than that I was only distantly aware of it. Comparatively, they and their feelings had ceased to be real.

I didn't normally behave like this. I can't remember it happening before. It wasn't that sort of a party, or the way these people carried on. They weren't particularly old-fashioned or principled people. They just didn't do it that way. Later, it was the way I had done it so openly in front of them and in front of Molly that shocked me, giving me the feeling that I was ceasing to be a person I could recognize.

At once, and though we were separated by several others who sipped and gnawed, we came together and walked into the trees. We held hands. We lay together and looked at the moon through the pine branches. We kissed and held on to each other.

We held each other with a relief that was like no other I had ever known. And with terror that they should separate us.

For me the relief was partly anticipation, because I knew that sooner or later I was going to tell her things which I had told no other person. I hoped it didn't matter, now that the time was so near. Whether it mattered or not I was going to tell her.

Their giggles and squeals drew us back to the pool. There was a splash and some wet flapping. Holding hands, we came through the trees and stood at the edge of the water, empty of people now, but still disturbed.

Behind and around us they were giggling and running in the darkness, though who they were I couldn't tell. They were in the shadows or passing quickly across patches of moonlight. A second later someone in a bathing costume hurtled past me. I never knew if they were pushed or ran. I think it was Janie but I never knew because at once they had landed heavily a few feet out and a curtain of water had risen over us.

We were drenched.

They stood round us, dabbing and apologizing. First there was Hubert, as if he had been watching. He wiped her dress with a towel and led her away to change. Suddenly I understood. Jeffy was Hubert's girl. As well as all the others who had watched us casually, he had been watching us specifically, knowing all the time where we were.

I wouldn't let them dry me. I said I wasn't wet, although my shirt and trousers were soaked and I was shivering. The party at the pool was over and I followed them to the house. No one tried to walk with me.

I would have liked to leave at once, but I couldn't bear to speak to Molly. I couldn't bear to admit that she was here.

They danced and became gay. Janie, dressed again, danced with her shoes off, kicking up her heels. She danced marvellously, making Charlie's thick stomach seem part of her dance. Jim danced with Molly. The Draycotts danced together, holding each other neatly. They were like mice on their hind legs. I sat in the doorway of the veranda, on a single seat where no one could join me.

Then I was watching again. I was watching Mrs. Willis.

There she sat, wearing that hussar's hat, like a pantomime principal boy, showing that coy fringe of blue rinse above her white, bloodless face with its powder-filled valleys. Again I was being astonished at my obtuseness.

What were these bridge parties she was supposed to give, though I had never met anyone who played with her? Why did they go on so late? What was this story about gin bottles put out each morning, when I had never seen her the smallest part drunk? Couldn't even remember her holding a drink.

The next moment my warning message had come back to me. 'H.Q.' It seemed so obvious. I was looking at H.Q. Her bridge parties, her secret meetings. Her drunkenness, an invented screen. I had been bothering myself with Wilfred, Charlie, Jim, trying to decide which of them mattered most. They mattered equally and hardly at all. They were the creatures of Mrs. Willis.

I stared at her with horror and hatred. Strangely, what made me most angry was not this new evil power I had discovered in her but the fact that she was still here, alive when she ought not to be. More alarming, as I stared at her she turned her grey chicken's neck and saw me. In that instant recognition passed between us.

I had to leave. As soon as the dance finished I found Molly and we said good-bye.

'Oh, don't go,' Janie said, putting her arms round Molly, trying to walk her back.

'We won't let them,' Jim said, shaking my hand and keeping it in his big grip.

For a second I thought that others were moving forward, about to close behind me and jostle me back. They would be playful but they wouldn't let me pass. 'I must . . .' I said. I controlled myself, hearing my panic. 'It's late.'

The music changed and Janie took Jimmy to dance. 'Let 'em go,' she said. 'They don' like our parties.'

She danced away from us, not looking back, and for a moment we hesitated in the doorway. Across the party I saw Jeffy for the first time since the garden. She was standing alone against a far wall and saw me but didn't wave. I understood nothing.

The Brightworths' drive was lit grey by the high moon. It was only two nights from full. So was ours when we crossed the New Lane. Ahead I saw a lighted window in our house. I wanted to run. It showed me how my nerves were in pieces. I clenched my fists and walked steadily towards it.

We never left lights burning when we were out, to frighten burglars. I had more respect for burglars' intelligences.

For thirty seconds we went like this. I was sure from the way she didn't mention it that Molly had seen it and was also astonished. By the time we reached the lawn I'd realized it was Dan's light.

I hurried ahead up the stairs. He was in bed reading.

'Hallo.'

'Hallo,' he said. He was lying on his stomach, propped by his elbows, his chin in his hands.

'You reading?' I said.

'That's right,' he said.

It was better than I deserved.

'Been reading long?' I asked.

'I don't think so,' he said, turning his head to look at me. His conversation seemed odd, as if he was adjusting it to the curious things, by daylight standards, which adults seemed to say at one in the morning. I thought this might be frightening him.

Molly came past me and began to tell him we were home. I saw how she distracted him while gently taking and closing his book.

I wondered what had made him wake and read. I guessed he had been doing it for a long time, waiting for us. I went to Peggy's room. The door was open and the foot of her bed was lit by the landing light. She was asleep.

She was low in the bedclothes, not much of her showing. Because of this her head was tipped back and her face turned up, suggesting a fish coming to the surface. I bent and kissed her and she took a startled breath and let it out in a sigh.

All next morning I wondered what I should do. I walked about the house. I walked about the overcast garden. I went down the path to the orchards. Half-way, I stopped and came back. What alarmed me was the single day that was now left and the idea that I had had all the instructions I was going to have.

I had imagined that as the time came near I would be kept in closer touch. The opposite was happening. My head was bad again, and it wasn't the drink. The sense of swelling was acute and it seemed to half close my eyes. I didn't like to bend.

By the afternoon I knew what I must do. I waited till Molly was cooking, then took a trowel and trug. I crossed the lawn, sunny now after the dull morning, to a small herbaceous bed between the front drive and the tennis court. It was one Molly didn't attend to much. By the time she discovered – if she ever did . . .

I dug four roots of Michaelmas daisies, put them in the trug and smoothed the earth. I hid the trowel in the bushes.

After tea when Molly and the children were having a bonfire on the hillside I took the trug and went down the New Lane to Mrs. Willis's house.

I'd never been in it. Occasionally she'd come to our parties but she'd not invited us back. I guessed that she never invited anyone – if you didn't count her bridge parties. I had counted them, of course, that had been so clever. Her house was one of the ugliest in the lane, with grey stucco and chocolate paint and rectangular bay windows. It was unpretentious. It made no pretence to have been built at any other time than the thirties.

I stood on the porch, between windows edged in red glass, facing a front door of panels of frosted glass, and rang the bell. It was one of those bells which ring loudly immediately inside the door, making the bell push shudder.

There were steps in the house and the door opened. Inside were two girls. One was an ordinary girl standing several yards back in the passage. I saw her first because the other, holding the door, was a dwarf, so that I had to look a yard lower than I'd expected.

I remembered the art-student lodgers. Why hadn't Molly told me that one of them was a dwarf?

'Hallo,' I said.

'Hallo,' they said together.

'Is Mrs. Willis in?'

'Yes, please,' the dwarf girl said. She had a strong foreign accent. She didn't move out of the doorway or offer to fetch her.

'Could I speak to her?' I asked.

The dwarf turned to the other girl. If some message passed between them I missed it. 'We don't think so,' the other girl said.

I understood. Though it was now five o'clock she still wasn't dressed. I cursed myself for my impatience – or was this something they had been trained to say, whatever the time of day?

'Never mind,' I said. 'I'll call back.'

I wasn't going to hand them the trug though I'd seen their eyes straying to it. To think of one reason for calling had been hard enough. 'I expect she's not up yet.'

'It isn't that,' the girl said.

Again the dwarf looked at her, as if anxious about what she might say.

'We think she's ill.'

'Oh dear,' I said, politely interested. I was more than that.

'When we took her tea . . .' the girl said, and hesitated. 'She wouldn't answer the door. She couldn't speak properly.'

I watched them sharply, but now they both looked at me.

'You should call a doctor,' I said.

'We were discussing,' the dwarf said.

'When you rang,' the girl said.

At this point I would have taken a step forward but the dwarf stayed in the doorway.

'We couldn't find her nightdress,' the girl said.

'You mean she was dressed?' I said.

Without saying anything or nodding they seemed to agree.

'She may not have one,' the girl said.

'I doubt that,' I said.

'It could be at the laundry,' the girl said, but not hopefully.

'She would haaf two,' the dwarf said. 'Two more,' she said, making herself clear.

'Certainly,' I said, becoming increasingly worried by this discussion which I seemed unable to stop.

I put down my trug. 'You must call the doctor at once,' I said. 'It may be urgent.'

They still hesitated, the dwarf holding the door with one hand raised from her shoulder to about the level of my stomach. Her hand was adult size. In the darkness of the hall, beyond the other girl, I could now see the telephone with its money box.

'Haaf you pennies?' the dwarf said.

'She charges us fourpence,' the other girl said, as if it was a mild grievance, though she was unsure whether this was the moment to mention it.

'Don't worry about that,' I said, stepping forward. The dwarf took her arm down and let me come. I noticed how indefinitely they were behaving, as if we had reached an unrehearsed part of the scene.

I was close to the other girl before she started and held out her hand. I counted the pennies into it. Even then she hesitated, but I didn't move till she had turned to the telephone and lifted the receiver.

At once I went past her and climbed the stairs. In three long strides I reached the top. Below I could see the dwarf coming after me. She climbed with enormous muscular effort, jerking her body backwards to lift her feet as high as her thighs. It was as if she were getting up a series of four-foot terraces.

I opened two doors on empty bedrooms and then the right one.

I'd noticed the smell when I'd stood on the porch, coming out at me in startling breaths, and then strong and choking as soon as I was in the hall. It was cat, I thought, but so fresh that there was ammonia with it. The door I now opened let out the same smell, but warmer and mixed with other things like mothballs. I hesitated, reluctant to go in unless I could take a deep breath and hold it. I might be sick.

The room was a grey confusion. Garments which I couldn't identify and didn't want to look at lay about the floor. One curtain was drawn, making it dark even on this sunny afternoon.

Mrs. Willis lay on the bed. She was flat on her back except her head, which was propped forward at forty-five degrees by a pillow. A blanket covered her to the chest and her hands were holding the edge of this. They looked grey. Her eyes were open and they watched the door.

They seemed to watch the door – it wasn't till I'd moved a pace forward into the room, my stomach rising, that I noticed they hadn't followed. I saw the cunning of that: they could see but pretend never to have seen.

'Mrs. Willis,' I said.

The third time I said it she groaned.

'I've brought you some daisies,' I said. 'Michaelmas,' I added quickly.

Watching her closely I thought her eyes took on a look of incomprehension.

'They're from my wife,' I went on. 'Molly.' I wasn't taking any chances. If she could be cunning, so could I. 'I left them downstairs when I heard from your lodgers . . .'

The door behind me was opening. The dwarf stood there. She didn't speak, as if she might be out of breath from her ascent. She stood as she had stood at the house door, one hand stretched up, but this time set against the door post, like some small-scale giant pausing before she shoved it over. It was the room's only door.

I had to get out of that horrible room. Soon something would happen to make this impossible. In one or perhaps two seconds . . . I pushed roughly past her and reached the landing.

She made no attempt to stop me. Perhaps she knew she couldn't – or saw that I had recognized my danger in time. I began to drop down the stairs in threes.

So quickly had it happened that I could hear below me the girl in the hall still trying to reach the doctor. 'Hallo,' she was saying. 'Are you there?' As I came dropping towards her I was aware of the stairs growing darker and saw beyond her the front door of the house closing. I understood why the dwarf hadn't moved.

I jumped the last six stairs. I gripped at the door's edge with my fingers, but I had underestimated its strength. The strong spring tore it from them and it slammed.

One thing saved me, the belief that I still had that second of advantage when I had seen my danger before they'd expected. I turned back into the hall and bounded past the girl at the telephone.

I saw her startled face. 'Oh, doctor,' she had begun. She stopped, stood upright, but didn't leave the telephone. The next moment I was beyond the bend, had passed through a door and turned the key behind me.

I stood panting. There wasn't a sound in the house, that was the most alarming thing. It was as if the door I had locked was perfectly insulated. Then, faintly, I could hear voices. I thought they might be close on the door's far side.

I was in the kitchen. I took off my shoes and crossed between kitchen table and cooker. I passed through the scullery and tested a door. It opened. That open door frightened me more than anything yet, but there seemed no choice. I went quickly through it and stood against the outside wall.

I was on a small shaded piece of path. The bushes were twelve feet away. I braced myself for the dash I must make. I glanced at the ground, looking perhaps for a good push-off. I saw a flash of white. I bent and snatched it.

I read, 'One pint today please. Then none till SATURDAY.'

I said it to myself three times. I set it back where I had found it. Things were happening so fast that I only then realized that it had been held in place by three square, green gin bottles.

I launched myself across that gap with its single ray of yellowing sunlight and in two seconds was on my knees, breathless among the laurels. I noticed that I was still holding my shoes. There was no time to tie them now. I made a fast low crossing behind her house and struck the New Lane thirty yards above her gate.

I was still carrying them when I came into my back drive. Something must have slipped in my mind. I hesitated.

'Hallo,' a voice said. I looked here and there but could see nothing. Sweat drenched me. Terrifyingly, it was a voice I recognized. A child's voice . . .

'Where have you been?'

It was Dan. He came down a low tree, where I suppose he'd been playing by himself at Indians. He stood up to his knees in heather, watching me.

I stared at him. As if by instinct, I raised a finger to my lips, winked and went quietly up the drive. I could feel him watching me.

Half an hour later as I stood in the veranda, the late evening sunlight coming in a yellow glare through the window at one end, I saw someone approaching up the front drive. Perhaps it was the sunlight which prevented me seeing at once who it was. They were close before I recognized the art student girl and saw that she was carrying my trug of Michaelmas daisies.

She stopped on the lawn. 'You left this,' she said.

'Thanks.' I hurried forward and took it.

I wished she'd go, but she stood there as if she hadn't finished. Behind me, through the sitting-room, I heard a door slam. To my right Molly was coming round the corner of the house.

'He's been,' the girl said.

'The doctor?' I said, hurrying her. 'What did he say?'

'Nothing much,' she said. 'That's the trouble.'

'What's the trouble?' Molly said, but instead of looking at the girl she began to stare in a fixed way at my trug.

'If only he'd tell us,' the girl said.

'It's Mrs. Willis,' I explained to Molly. 'She's ill.'

'Who's ill?' Peggy said from behind me at the sitting-room french windows.

'Whatever have you got there?' Molly said.

I was worried by the way she wouldn't take it casually, but went on staring at it as if she found it very disturbing, as if she would have liked to treat it as a joke but didn't dare.

'A present,' I said vaguely.

'We're doing our best to look after her,' the girl said. She seemed about to cry.

'Who?' Peggy said, in that nervous insistent way she used when she scented an adult secret about illness or death.

'No one,' Molly said. 'Mrs. Willis,' I said, both at the same moment.

While we were saying these things Dan had come round the other corner of the house to stand on the lawn. He stared at my shoes, which I was now wearing, and then at me. He gave several large winks. He hadn't learnt to wink easily and did them in sudden jerks, screwing up his mouth and most of one side of his face.

I turned and went into the sitting-room. Between the sofa

and armchair I stopped. I was still carrying my trug. 'Wasn't that the telephone,' I said desperately. I put down the trug and went straight through the house and out by the back door.

I went down the pathway to the low lands and my orchards.

Those were the last calm moments I had, down there among my fruit trees. The fruit was heavy on them and hung undisturbed in the quiet summer evening. The sun was on their tops though I was walking in shadow. Far away I could hear noises, twice of car engines and once of children shouting.

As I climbed again I met our cat on the path. It stood by itself, watching me, and when I came close it arched its back to rub itself against my shins. I didn't want to let it. Then I let it.

The sun was setting when I reached the house. From the back drive I could see it, a great red ball between the pines low over the hills. I went through the sitting-room – the trug had gone – and upstairs. I could hear them having supper in the kitchen. I went into our bedroom. It had been searched.

It hadn't been done violently or hurriedly but carefully and thoroughly. Everything was a little different. If I hadn't been looking for it I might not have noticed.

To start with, three of the drawers were half an inch from fully shut. Inside the top left one my pile of handkerchiefs was on its side. The pillows were disturbed, and the telephone had been set with the dial facing the bedside mat, not the bed, as I always kept it. And several rolls of dust had come from under the furniture on to the carpet, as if they had been blown there when the bed was stripped or remade.

I stood at the top of the stairs and shouted as loud as I could, 'Who's been up here?' I could hear my voice echoing about the house. I could hear how it sounded frightened as well as angry.

I wanted to go away and pretend I hadn't done it but that wasn't possible now. I had to stand there, imagining their shock, hearing their chairs go back in succession as they started to come, thinking I must be playing some game. I heard Molly tell them to stay. That would frighten them more.

Then she was in the hall. 'What is it?' Their heads followed her round the kitchen doorway.

'Doesn't matter,' I said. I turned as if I'd had some more important idea. 'I wondered if the children had been messing around,' I said, still facing away.

'In our bedroom?' she asked.

After a pause I said, 'That's right.'

'I changed up there,' she said.

It was true, she was wearing a skirt instead of slacks. At once I realized how clever they had been. The drawers not fully closed, as she often left them; the telephone turned from the bed as if she'd made a call; the pillows and the dust.

I should never have let my shock show. There was nothing in the bedroom they could find. I moved away from the stairhead. Below I heard her go back to the kitchen. 'Your supper's waiting.'

I think I'd been shocked to realize that they could come inside, too. I'd never imagined that.

I didn't sleep that night. After several hours my mind began to drift into fantasy as it often did when I was near to sleep. At that moment I remembered meaning to put my .38 with the silencer between the mattresses on the night there'd been someone in the garden. I hadn't thought of it since.

I could remember the moment of meaning to do it. I could remember thinking there was still time to fetch it. I couldn't remember what I'd done.

I could remember the problem of how far to push it under, so that it wouldn't fall out but would be easy to reach; or was that only a problem I'd foreseen?

Very carefully I worked my hand out between the sheets, then back between the mattresses. It wasn't there.

I was wide awake now, my heart pounding. But I had to lie still. While I was feeling I'd heard Molly move. I listened for her breathing but couldn't hear it. When she was asleep it grew regular and a little louder. As I listened, by association I had a panic about my own breathing and at that moment felt my heart stop. I had time to wonder whether it would start again before it was thumping fast as if to make up what it had lost. Though I lay only under a sheet I was soaked.

There had been no cooling at sunset. The night felt airless, as if the soft clouds of the morning had come back after dark and wrapped in the heat. Tomorrow the moon would be full, the harvest moon, and it should have been bright moonlight, the brightest of the year; but the grey square of window didn't seem like that.

I must have lain still for an hour, wondering why she didn't fall asleep. Twice I heard her sigh. Every sound I heard made me break into a new wash of sweat. I began to shiver. Suppose they had been disturbed at their work and had to hide. Suppose they were still hidden in the house? The owls were hooting, but far away down on the common. I slipped out of bed.

For a minute I crouched, waiting for her to speak. I could have said I was using the pot. I went with soft steps out of the bedroom on to the landing. I went into the bathroom and took off my pyjamas and rubbed myself hard with a towel.

I began to walk about the house, but I didn't know where I was going. I used a torch at first and went quietly. I stood in doorways, wondering where to go next. Sometimes I discovered myself standing and wasn't sure how long I'd been there.

I thought of going to the cellar to check my guns. I knew better than to do that when every movement I made could be watched.

The black rooms of the house began to frighten me and I switched on lights. I went quickly round the house switching on every light. It seemed important to do this at once. I noticed my toe was bleeding. I hadn't felt a thing. I thought of the house as it would seem from the garden, all its lights shining out into the night. That would show them.

I was coming up the stairs. I think I was talking to myself, but I don't remember what I was saying. I was worried by this bright light and the way I was walking about so conspicuously at its centre. More and more it seemed to be directed at me and I wanted to escape from it. Glancing up, I saw Molly at the head of the stairs.

She stood in her long white nightdress, staring at me. 'What's happening?'

'I couldn't sleep.'

'The lights . . .' I noticed she was shivering, not just her arms but her jaw and whole face. 'Why are they on?'

'Are they?' I said, cunning again, but there seemed little point. It was then that I felt real anger with her, anger at the way she was interfering and making my task more difficult.

'You must come to bed.'

I stared at her, trying to hide my anger which was close to hatred. I managed to shrug my shoulders. I went round the house turning off the lights. I went to bed. As I passed the landing clock I saw it was twelve-thirty. I'd imagined it must be three at least.

All night I lay awake. The clouds went away and I could see the bright moonlight on the pine tops in the garden. Dawn came and I lay still, putting off the moment when I would get up. It was the waiting I couldn't bear. There would be nothing to do but wait. Perhaps I fell into a doze. I turned and Molly had gone. I didn't remember her going.

I dressed quickly. At once I knew what I had to do – and do quickly.

I had let myself be frightened into evasion – though I hadn't for a moment been deceived. Her mock illness, so cleverly contrived. It must have been contrived in the few seconds after they had seen me coming up the path – or had she expected me ever since that look we had exchanged at the party?

I could hardly wait for breakfast to finish.

The excuse was no problem. I would go to inquire about her health. I was working out the details, filling time by a circuit of the house, when I saw, just outside the backdoor, my trug of Michaelmas daisies. Should I take them too? Then if she was still ill I could offer to plant them. Left out of the earth much longer, they would die. It would give me a perfect reason for a careful survey of the garden. I hesitated. Some memory about the ritual associations of Michaelmas daisies was worrying me. I heard a car in the front drive.

I stepped into shadow. I went through the back door and stood listening in the scullery. There were voices on the lawn. Their voices drew me through the house. It was Dr. Grott.

I saw him from the sitting-room door, standing between the sofa and the french windows, talking to Molly. Though I couldn't see his features against the light, I knew it was he by his tallness and the silhouette of his short stiff hair which was like a brush. When he saw me he said, 'How are we keeping?' in that friendly but guarded way doctors use, in case there will be bad news to break soon.

I wanted to ask him angrily why he'd come. Who could have called him when no one was ill? I wanted to drive him out.

He turned back to Molly and went on with something he was saying – about Dan I guessed because I could now see him beyond them on the lawn, coming nearer with half untucked shirt. I remembered his rash.

'Dr. Grott dropped in so I thought he'd better look at Dan,' Molly said.

'Dropped in!' I said. But if they noticed my sarcasm they pretended not to.

'He's just been down there.' She gestured with her head. She glanced to see how close Dan had come. 'Mrs. Willis,' she said quietly. 'She's died.'

My astonished horror must have shown. I think it surprised them.

'Heart,' Molly said.

'Seventy-seven,' Dr. Grott said.

'We were just wondering,' Molly said, 'if you'd let Dr. Grott give you a check-up?'

'Me?' I said.

'Well, all of us,' Molly said. 'We ought to be,' she hurried on. 'Everyone should be. Every year.' She sat in an armchair, her head a little back, as if offering herself to be checked. 'That's why Dr. Grott came.'

'But you didn't say that,' I said. 'You said it was because of Mrs. Willis.'

'Well, now he's here,' Molly said, but less hopefully, as if already admitting defeat. 'Please.'

She had stood again. She was appealing to me. And suddenly I had an idea that she was appealing about something different. She was asking me to understand this, or if I didn't understand it, to trust her. The fear and anxiety in her eyes were so terrible that I hesitated. Perhaps it was this which encouraged them both to begin to move forward. I saw Dr. Grott's hands come up. I hesitated so long that his hands actually started to feel the glands at the base of my neck.

'No,' I shouted. I hurried away from them.

At the moment I felt his hands and saw Molly watching beside him, my understanding had become complete. It didn't matter where I started: with the moment I had met her crossing to the Draycotts with the jar of *pâté,* or the time I had found her coming down our drive on the way to that gathering at the Brightworths'. If I ignored the footprint in the flower-bed and the way it had been covered up, there was the way she had tested me by asking why we no longer quarrelled.

The calling of the policemen, the unnecessary tennis party, the stealing of my gun, her attitude to my telephone calls, the moment as far back as the day of the stand-by when I'd seen her on the way to my attic, all pointed in the same direction.

And now the way she had helped them so ruthlessly to do away with the old woman as soon as she was suspect and called the doctor to explain it to me. And tried to tempt me . . . I went to the bedroom and lay on our bed. There was something shocking yet totally foreseeable about what I was to be asked to do. It was the hardest thing of all and so the most likely. I realized that on a certain level I had always thought about this possibility. I could afford to because it hadn't seemed possible.

I could hear my children playing on the tennis court. Outside my north window there was grey shadow, but there on the other side of the house they were shouting to each other in the sun. I sat upright, worried by the tears which were running down my face.

Unlike the others whom I had suspected and at once hated for the vicious deceit of their lives, I could not hate Molly. I loved her more. That was why, for the first time, I was certain.

PART SEVEN

THAT afternoon the order came. All day I'd expected it but when it came it wasn't the order I'd expected. I didn't know what it meant.

As soon as I heard the doctor go I got up from my bed. I had to force myself to do it. Suddenly I was tired. I only wanted to go on lying there. I had to tell myself that there were only a few more efforts now.

But I had to go slowly. I was feeling my lack of sleep as I hadn't before. When I made sudden movements my heart pounded and sometimes as I walked carefully or stood listening I seemed to be losing my balance and raised my arms sideways, thinking I was falling when I wasn't. Presently I started to follow her.

At first I followed her at a distance – just to be sure I always knew where she was. When she was upstairs I stood in the hall, listening to her moving up there. When she went into the garden I stood in the veranda, sometimes taking a step forward so that I could see her, sometimes stepping back into the shadows.

At lunch I couldn't talk. I couldn't eat. I took my plate to the sink and put the food into the bin, pretending I'd finished it. After lunch I followed her more closely.

I was frightened that she might make a sudden run. That was why I had to follow her closely. But I was frightened, too, that she might notice. Several times I thought she glanced back anxiously as I waited just out of the line of a doorway she'd gone through. And once she came out quickly again, surprising me. 'Oh!' she said with a sort of gasp and shudder, but went on quickly as if it was nothing she could explain.

It was after tea – I hadn't had any. I watched her carry the tray into the kitchen then go upstairs to the bathroom. I followed her there, then went up the flight to my attic. After a few steps I stopped and kept still. Peering back and down I could tell she was still there by the slight changes of light her shadow kept making on the landing. Then I saw Dan and Peggy. They were on the lower stairs where they must have followed us. They were both staring at me with wide eyes. I saw that Peggy was about to ask what on earth I was doing, standing there so curiously, leaning back and peering down over my shoulder. 'It's not true,' I wanted to shout at them. 'I'm not doing it.' I ran the last steps up to my attic. That was when I got the order.

I heard it as soon as I opened the door. It was coming from below the floorboards and went on steadily, as if humming to itself. Perhaps it had been doing it all day.

It must have switched itself on, using some emergency procedure I didn't know about. I leapt for my pad and pencil. I squatted by the boards, ready to decode the message which it would begin to send at any moment. Instead it went on humming with a steady beat. 'Wow wow wow wow wow wow.' There's no other way to describe it.

I lifted the boards. I worked the knobs. I made it louder, then softer – though I could never quite make it disappear. I could get no other sound.

What could it mean?

It was like someone beating the air, only they would never have had time to raise their arm. It was like something flapping. Wings. Butterflies.

No doubt I'd got used to their messages, stripped to their essentials, but I couldn't help a moment's pride at my skill. It wasn't this which kept me on my knees for fifteen seconds more, but relief that it wasn't the order which I had been expecting all day. There were tears of gratefulness in my eyes. I stared at the equipment between the floor joists, wishing there was something I dared do to thank them.

Anger came later. I was in the woods, working myself up a gully of dry leaves and snapping twigs towards the kitchen garden and beyond it that circle of lawn which I had looked at through my binoculars from the hills ten miles to the east on the day of our picnic. It was anger with myself, of course, for not seeing through the transparent double bluff. But mostly it was anger with this bogus lepidopterist.

Though I still believed that he was the centre of some organization in which the Draycotts, Quorum, all of them, yes, even Molly, were involved, I began to understand that it was an organization unlike any I had suspected. Because it was no organization. It had none of the secret-meeting, coded-message character which I had suspected. It wasn't a cell for the dissemination of propaganda. They were involved with him in a way they none of them perhaps knew about because of their love for him. He was their leader because of what he was.

To them he represented compassion, that supreme quality overflowing into universal love, which they none of them possessed but all longed for. It was compassion that I was to destroy, with its head-in-the-sand escapist fallacy.

By destroying it – try as I would to avoid the question, my logic led me to it – whose side would I be acting on? Creeping forward up that crackling ditch I crushed the thought.

The wood went on a long way – why had I never wondered that his house should be surrounded by so large a wood? It grew thicker, with tangled brambles and low branches between the trees which blocked my path. Although I knew it was still bright daylight outside, it seemed here like evening already. I began to hear noises which weren't mine in the trees around me. I should have expected it.

They grew louder and closer to me as I hurried forward. I began to tear my clothes on the brambles and once fell into a leaf-filled hole. Twice I stopped, half in panic, half because the undergrowth had blocked me. I stood still, shivering and listening. All around there was silence, as if they had stopped at the same instant.

I began to run towards any brighter light I could see through the trees, not caring where I came out so long as I escaped from this wood. Each time I seemed to lose the brightness and looked round in panic for some new direction to try. The footsteps were closer as if no longer caring how much noise they made. The scream was rising in my throat – when I saw the trees thinning ahead and came out into the low evening sunlight. I crouched and ran between shrubs, my legs brushing through heather. I could tell from how low the sun had sunk how much time I had wasted in the wood.

As soon as I could see the red roof and imitation Tudor chimneys I stopped for breath. I must check that in my scramble through the woods I had dropped nothing. I felt in my pocket. It was still there.

Ever since I'd got the message I'd known I couldn't bear him to be facing me. I could not bear the idea of his eyes watching me as I aimed at his stomach, and of how they would fill with pain when the first shot hit him. I had to manage it differently.

Once I hesitated as I made my way up the side of his vegetable garden, using the beech hedge for cover, only ten feet from where I'd worked two days before. I got the idea that he'd known what was going to happen. It would explain why he'd wanted me to prune his blackcurrants: so that I could see the approaches. It fitted with all I knew and hated about him. I hurried forward among the rhododendrons.

Peering through them I could see directly on to the circle of lawn. Not more than five or six yards away, at the edge of his veranda, Percy was sitting in a deckchair. He was facing away from me, bathed in the yellow evening sunlight. He had a book on his knees, but I thought from its angle that he was asleep.

I got out the cord and adjusted the knot. I moved along the bushes and began to creep forward in the open. Though I was in the open for these first yards I was hidden by the near end wall of the veranda. Only for the last two would I be in full view if he heard me and turned. I'd reached these and was staring past him at the far windows of the veranda when without warning I was crouching and shivering. I had begun to hunt again.

And now I didn't care whether or not I should let myself hunt. I didn't care that I was making my memories real when they might not be. To me they were real because they were the only reality I had. And this was the last moment I had. I swept them all aside in the hunt for the one memory which I realized for days now I had been trying to recover, a memory of something which had really happened and I had not invented or contrived. I seemed to grasp at it. It was like a voice, the voice of a real person speaking to me. In my memory it grew more and more substantial till it was on the point of appearing, solid and visible. There it was. There could no longer be any doubt. My mind choked on the words. They were the opposite of the truth. There could only be doubt . . .

At that moment I saw Percy's peke.

I saw it clearly, where it must have been lying all the time, by the far corner post of the veranda, also in the sun. Its ear had twitched.

It had its rump towards me and its head towards the drive, no doubt so that it could yap at visitors without getting to its feet. Because of the way it was lying I couldn't tell whether it was asleep or had its eyes open, ranging over its field of view.

I thought of going back and inventing a new plan. I thought of rushing and hoping. Neither was any good. Very cautiously I began to move forward again. At that exact second its ear twitched.

I was so sure I'd made no noise that I thought it must be coincidence. I had to think so. I went on moving forward, an inch at a time, holding the cord in front of me, the knot in my right hand, my left keeping the loop open.

He was wearing an open shirt, and its collar had fallen back so that his neck showed to where it joined his shoulders. The top of his neck was brown and wrinkled, the bottom white and smooth. There was a clear line.

Glancing down I opened my right hand to see that the knot seemed free. I judged the size of the loop and glanced up to see that it seemed big enough for his head. Beyond his head I saw that the peke had risen on its fore-feet and was staring at me.

Astonishment must have silenced it for that vital second. I jumped.

The noose was tight before he seemed to feel it. If he made any sound it was drowned by the peal of yaps the peke had begun and I had the strange idea that he, too, was distracted by this.

His hands came up and began to feel at the cord, trying to get inside it, but they didn't try hard and presently fell away. I saw them hanging by the side of the deckchair, opening and shutting.

I pulled as hard as I could with my right hand, at the same time forcing the knot forward with my left. I was worried by the indefiniteness of what I was doing, but determined to go on as long as necessary. I think it was the sight of his hands opening and shutting that upset me. The deckchair fell sideways and he sat on the ground.

But I still held the cord. I began to notice how his face was turning purple. I knew that his eyes would be swelling out of his head. Suddenly I was angry. Why wouldn't he die? I put my foot on his shoulder and pulled with all my strength. The cord broke.

At the instant this happened I imagined that he would rise slowly to his feet and turn to face me. I was petrified. With relief I saw him roll on to his side and heard his head hit the brick of the veranda.

I ran. I'd always known I'd have to hurry once the job was done. I'd have to behave as if I thought I'd escape, however little I expected to. That wasn't how I ran. I ran with panic. Something had happened which I didn't understand.

I ran through the woods and out on to the New Lane. I came running in at our front gate. Molly was in the drive. I hadn't expected that. I stopped, realizing with horror that I was still holding the broken end of the cord.

'I heard something,' she said.

It muddled me. I didn't know what to say.

'It was like someone crying,' she said.

I turned to stare with her up the drive. I was imagining Percy at the gate, his face purple, his eyes coming out of his head. Then I couldn't see him but only the moon, round and full in the evening sky above the trees. I ran past her towards the house.

I ran to the attic and lifted the floorboards. There was no sound. The beating hum had stopped. I gave the call-up signal. I gave it several times. There was no answer. What did it mean?

I ran to the bedroom telephone and used the call-up procedure reserved for class one emergencies. No one answered.

I got out the escape clothes. That was what I had to do. However much I was shivering with panic I must carry out the routine. I put on the alpaca jacket and grey check sponge-bag trousers. As I struggled with them I noticed that I'd started to make a thin, whimpering noise like a dog shut in a room. I put on the suède shoes but my hands were shaking too much to tie them. After my second attempt to set the moustache there was glue up my nose.

There was no time to do better. I'd heard a door shut in the house below. Grabbing the panama hat, I hurried to the cellar.

I began to take the wine bottles out of the rack. The wall behind was blank. I began to put them back. I dropped a bottle and it broke. I stopped putting them back and began to take them from other racks. It was far too slow. I began to pull the complete racks away from the walls. I staggered against one and it toppled.

I pulled all the racks from all the walls. The walls were of plain grey brick. I trod among the bottles to get out of the cellar. I missed my footing and went on both hands and knees among the broken bottles. I felt their sharp glass edges. I stood up. My hat had come off and my moustache was crooked. There were dark wet patches on my trousers and my hands were dripping. Molly was at the top of the cellar steps.

I climbed towards her and she ran away screaming. Why was she running away from me like that? 'Stop,' I shouted but she ran out through the front door, leaving it open, across the drive and down the hillside. She stopped screaming on the drive but when she was jumping among the bushes ten yards down the hill she began again. She screamed with a continuous high squeal, like a pig I'd heard being killed illegally during the war. Why did she squeal like that? It made me very angry.

It also brought me to my senses. I took off the alpaca jacket and hung it in the hall. It could wait there for now. I got a wet towel and sponged the blood and wine off my trousers. There was a deep cut in one knee and the blood kept running into my sock.

There had been a mistake. Perhaps I had been too clever at interpreting that last message. Perhaps I had wanted to misinterpret it. Whatever it was, something had gone badly wrong. There had been an information leak too. How else could my transmitter have been interfered with and my cellar safe bricked up? Perhaps for many years there had been a continuous information leak so that everything I had done had been known and reported.

I fetched the panama and reset the moustache in the hall mirror. Now that I was warned there might still be time to undo what had been done so badly. I must wait now for their order which I had so impatiently anticipated. I thought I knew what it would be.

I couldn't hear her squealing any more. She had disappeared somewhere down the hillside in the dusk. Perhaps she had fallen.

It didn't matter. She would have to come back.

Francis King	To the Dark Tower
	Never Again
	An Air That Kills
	The Dividing Stream
	The Dark Glasses
	The Man on the Rock
C.H.B. Kitchin	Ten Pollitt Place
	The Book of Life
Hilda Lewis	The Witch and the Priest
Kenneth Martin	Aubade
	Waiting for the Sky to Fall
Michael Nelson	Knock or Ring
	A Room in Chelsea Square
Beverley Nichols	Crazy Pavements
Oliver Onions	The Hand of Kornelius Voyt
Dennis Parry	Sea of Glass
J.B. Priestley	Benighted
	The Other Place
	The Magicians
Peter Prince	Play Things
Piers Paul Read	Monk Dawson
Forrest Reid	The Garden God
	Following Darkness
	The Spring Song
	Brian Westby
	The Tom Barber Trilogy
	Denis Bracknel
David Storey	Radcliffe
	Pasmore
	Saville
Russell Thorndike	The Slype
	The Master of the Macabre
John Trevena	Sleeping Waters
John Wain	Hurry on Down
	The Smaller Sky
Keith Waterhouse	There is a Happy Land
	Billy Liar
Colin Wilson	Ritual in the Dark
	Man Without a Shadow
	The Philosopher's Stone
	The God of the Labyrinth

WHAT CRITICS ARE SAYING ABOUT VALANCOURT BOOKS

'Valancourt are doing a magnificent job in making these books not only available but – in many cases – known at all . . . these reprints are well chosen and well designed (often using the original dust jackets), and have excellent introductions.'

Times Literary Supplement (London)

'Valancourt Books champions neglected but important works of fantastic, occult, decadent and gay literature. The press's Web site not only lists scores of titles but also explains why these often obscure books are still worth reading. . . . So if you're a real reader, one who looks beyond the bestseller list and the touted books of the moment, Valancourt's publications may be just what you're searching for.'

Michael Dirda, *Washington Post*

'Valancourt Books are fast becoming my favourite publisher. They have made it their business, with considerable taste and integrity, to put back into print a considerable amount of work which has been in serious need of republication. If you ever felt there were gaps in your reading experience or are simply frustrated that you can't find enough good, substantial fiction in the shops or even online, then this is the publisher for you.'

Michael Moorcock

Lightning Source UK Ltd.
Milton Keynes UK
UKOW04f2315120116

266306UK00003B/129/P